Charles Reade, Tom Taylor

Masks and Faces

Charles Reade, Tom Taylor

Masks and Faces

ISBN/EAN: 9783337797409

Printed in Europe, USA, Canada, Australia, Japan

Cover: Foto ©Andreas Hilbeck / pixelio.de

More available books at **www.hansebooks.com**

MASKS AND FACES,

OR

BEFORE AND BEHIND THE CURTAIN

𝔄 𝔠𝔬𝔪𝔢𝔡𝔶.

IN TWO ACTS.

BY TOM TAYLOR, AND CHARLES READE,

Author of the King's Rival, &c., &c.

WITH EDITORIAL REMARKS, ORIGINAL CASTS, COSTUMES,

SCENE AND PROPERTY PLOTS,

AND ALL THE STAGE BUSINESS

———— • ————

NEW YORK:

SAMUEL FRENCH PUBLISHER

122 Nassau Street. (Up Stairs)

CAST OF CHARACTERS.

	Haymarket, London, 1852.	Adelphi, London, 1853.	Burton's, New York, 1853 & '54.	Howard, Boston, 1854.
Sir Charles Pomander......	Mr. Leigh Murray	Mr. Leigh Murray	Mr. G. Jordan	Mr. Warwick
Mr. Ernest Vane............	" Parselle	" Parselle	" Holman	" Loveday
Colley Cibber.............	" Lambert	G. Honey	" G. H. Barrett } " H. Russell }	" C. W. Hunt
Quin......................	Jas. Bland	Paul Bedford	" G. H. Andrews	Paullin
Triplet...................	Benj. Webster	Benj. Webster	" W. F. Burton } " C Fisher }	Wm. McFarland
Lysimachus Triplet........	Master Caulfield	Master Caulfield	Mast. Parslee	Mast. Paullin
Mr. Snarl.................	Mr. Stuart	Mr. O. Smith	Mr. Moore	Mr. Williams
" Soaper................	" Brald	" C. J. Smith	" Norton	" J. M. Cooke
James Burdock............	" Rogers	" R. Romer	" Radcliffe	" Seymour
Colander.................	" Clark	" Hastings	" Gourlay	" Adams
Hundsdon.................	" Coe	" Lindon	" Levere	" Powell
Call Boy.................	" Edwards	" Waye	" Lawson	" Bishop
Pompey...................	Mast. C. J. Smith	Mast. C. J. Smith	" Paul	Miss Mullen
Mrs. Vane................	Miss Rosa Bennett	Miss Woolgar	Mrs. Buckland	Miss F. Morant
Peg Woffington...........	Mrs. Stirling	Mad. Celeste	Miss C. Mitchell	" J. M. Davenport
Kitty Clive..............	Miss Maskell	Miss Maskell	Mrs. Holman	Mrs. Seymour
Mrs. Triplet.............	Mrs. Leigh Murray	Mrs Leigh Murray	Mrs. Hough	Miss Cutler
Roxalana.................	Miss Caulfield	Miss Caulfield	Miss Jansen	" Paullin
Maid.....................	" E. Weulds.	" Mitchenson	:: Jenkins	" Smith

Character	Walnut St., Philadelphia, 1854 & '55.	National, Boston, 1855.	Howard Steet, Boston, 1855	Broadway, New York, 1856.
Sir Charles Pomander	Mr. Perry	Mr. G W. Stoddart	Mr. W R. Floyd	Mr. Sandford
Mr. Ernest Vane	" Eytinge	" Lingham	" Blake	" Lazergan
Colley Cibber	" Stafford	" C. W. Hield	" W. H. Curtis	" Leffingwell
Quin	" Boswell	" Verney	" P. Jones	" France
Triplet	" A. Beckett	" L. P. Roys	" H. Farren	" Conway
Lysimachus Triplet	Mast. Reed	Mast. Paullin		Mast. Wallis
Mr. Snarl	Mr. Young	Mr. Paullin	Mr. Woodward	Mr Grosvenor
" Soaper	" Wallis	" Powell	" Ringold	" Seymour
James Burdock	" Eberle	" Pardey	" Adams	" Cutter
Colander	" Howard	" Lord	" Rose	" McDouall
Hundson	" Scallan	" Brown	" Guppy	" Vincent
Call Boy	Mast. Eberle	" Johnson	" Kendall	" Wallis
Pompey	" J. Reed	Mast. Mullin	" Wilson	
Mrs. Vane	Mrs. Duffield	Mrs. Cunningham	Miss Devlin	Miss A. Gougenhelm
Peg Woffington	{ Miss J. M. Davenport / " Weston	Md'lle Marie Duret	" Louisa Howard	" J. Gougenhelm
Kitty Clive	Mrs. King	Miss Julia Daly	Mrs. Marshall	Mrs. Seymour
Mrs. Triplet		Mrs. Hield	Miss "	" Nagle
Roxalana	Miss Folrode	Miss Paullin	" Florence	Miss Henry
Maid	" West			" Barnard

REMARKS.

This favorite comedy was first brought before the public at the Haymarket Theatre, London, under the title of Peg Woffington, and had a most successful run. Mrs. Stirling was all that could be wished as Peg; and the excellent part of James Triplet in the hands of Mr. Webster, was a most finished piece of acting. When Mr. Webster retired from the management of that theatre he produced it at the Adelphi, under the title of MASKS AND FACES, — where Madam Celeste sustained the part of Peg Woffington. It was first performed in this country at Burton's Theatre, New York, and met with decided approbation: Miss Charlotte Mitchell from the Lyceum Theatre, London, made her debut as Peg — and made a hit, and has since played the same character with considerable success at Albany, Buffalo, Cleveland, &c. The piece was well played throughout, embracing the strength of Burton's *Star* Company. MASKS AND FACES has since been produced by Miss Davenport, Miss Weston, and others in the various cities of the Union, and has invariably proved successful. Last season, it was revived at the Howard Athenæum, Miss Louisa Howard playing the mischievous, but kindhearted Peg to perfection; and Mr. Henry Farren's James Triplet was a truthful delineation of character. (This gentleman possesses the requisites of a good actor, and only requires to be more often seen to be highly appreciated by the American public.) We predict for MASKS AND FACES a brilliant success, wherever it may be presented.

SCENERY.

ACT ONE.

SCENE 1 — Green Room of the theatre, 2 G.

SCENE 2 — An elegant apartment, 4 and 7 G. French windows in flat R. and L. Lattice C. doors open, backed with garden flats. Garden cloth down from 4th to 7th G. painted with walks and flower beds. Set statues, flower pieces, and small trees. Set door, 2 E. R. H. Set door, 3 E. L. H. Quick drop.

ACT TWO.

SCENE 1 — Rude garret, 3 G. Window in flat C. practical, backed by horizon and tops of houses. Set door 2 E. R. H. Set door 2 E. L. H.

PROPERTIES

ACT ONE.

SCENE 1 -- Green cloth down. Plain table and 2 chairs on R. C. Call wafered on looking glass in flat C. Call-book for Call-Boy. Walking cane and jewelled snuff-box for Sir Charles — Written letter and part for Peg. Portrait of Peg. (face to be cut out in act 2.) covered with green baize, and no frame. Several manuscripts tied up in brown paper, ready L. 1 E. for Call-Boy.

SCENE 2 — Handsome round table C. covered. On it two fruit dishes with oranges, apples, two decanters of sherry and port wine, eight wine glasses, eight small plates, eight dessert knives, plate of toast, plate of biscuits, napkins. Side-table on L. with set of silver plate. Handsome sofa on R. H. Salver with rich coffee cups, and coffee, and spoons for servant. Salver with rich tea cups and tea spoons for servant. Salver with sealed letters for Burdock. Diamond snuff-box and snuff and eye-glasses with ribbons for Cibber. Portfolio, two volumes, roll of MSS. and a card for Triplet. Eight high backed chairs on, about stage R. and L.

ACT TWO.

SCENE 1 — Green cloth taken up. Old arm chair on R. H. Easel with Peg Woffington's portrait on it. (Up L. C. 3 G.) concealed by a green baize. Table on R. H. against flat, with Pallet Maulstick, colors, pencils and pallet knife, knives, forks, table cloth, wine glasses, violin hung on wall. Cradle L. C. 2 G. Small table in C 1 G. Pen, ink and paper, roll of MSS. Two rude chairs on, money for Peg, burnt cork for Pompey, written letter for maid. Handle (small) basket, with bottle of wine for Pompey. Apple pie ready 2. E. L. H. for Pompey. Cane, hood, and cardinal, and mask for Mabel.

☞ For Costume, see page 59.

MASKS AND FACES.

ACT I.

SCENE I. 2. G.—*The Green Room of the Theatre Royal, Covent Garden. A Fire-place c., with a Looking-glass over it, on which a call is wafered. Curtain rises on Mr. Quin and Mrs. Clive seated each side of Fire-place.*

Clive. Who dines with Mr. Vane to-day besides ourselves?

Quin. His inamorata, Mrs. Woffington, of this theatre.

Clive. Of course. But who else?

Quin. Sir Charles Pomander. The critics, Snarl and Soaper, are invited, I believe.

Clive. Then I shall eat no dinner.

Quin. Pooh! There is to be a haunch that will counterpoise in one hour a century of censure. Let them talk! the mouth will revenge the ears of Falstaff; — besides, Snarl is the only ill-natured one — Soaper praises people, don't he?

Clive. Don't be silly, Quin! Soaper's praise is only a pin for his brother executioner to hang abuse on : by this means Snarl, who could not invent even ill-nature, is never at a loss. Snarl is his own weight in wormwood; but Soaper is — hush! — hold your tongue.

Enter SNARL *and* SOAPER L. 1 E. QUIN *and* CLIVE *rise.*

(CLIVE, *with engaging sweetness.*) Ah! Mr. Snarl! Mr. Soaper! we were talking of you.

Snarl.   I am sorry for that, madam.

Quin.   We hear you dine with us at Mr. Vane's.

Soap.   We have been invited, and are here to accept I was told Mr. Vane was here.

Quin.   No; but he is on the stage.

Snarl.   Come, then, Soaper.   (*They move towards* L. 1 E.)

Soap.   (*Aside.*)   Snarl!

Snarl.   Yes.   (*With a look of secret intelligence.*)

Soap.   (*Crosses slowly to* CLIVE.)   My dear Mrs. Clive, there was I going away without telling you how charmed I was with your Flippanta; all that sweetness and womanly grace, with which you invested that character, was —

Snarl.   Misplaced.   Flippanta is a vixen, or she is nothing at all.

Soap.   Your Sir John Brute, sir, was a fine performance: you never forgot the gentleman even in your cups.

Snarl.   Which, as Sir John Brute is the exact opposite of a gentleman, he ought to have forgotten.   (*Exit* L.)

Soap.   But you must excuse me now; I will resume your praise at dinner-time.   (*Exit, with bows,* L.)

Clive.   (*Walks in a rage.*)   We are the most unfortunate of all artists.   Nobody regards our feelings.   (*Quin shakes his head.*)

Enter CALL-BOY, L.

Call-Boy.   Mr. Quin and Mrs. Clive!   (*Exit* CALL-BOY, L.)

Quin.   I shall cut my part in this play.

Clive.   (*Yawns.*)   Cut it as deep as you like, there will be enough left; and so I shall tell the author if he is there.

(*Exeunt* QUIN *and* CLIVE, L.)

Enter MR. VANE *and* SIR CHARLES POMANDER, L.

Pom.   All this eloquence might be compressed into one word — you love Mrs. Margaret Woffington.

Vane.   I glory in it.

Pom.   Why not, if it amuses you?   We all love an actress once in our lives, and none of us twice.

Vane. You are the slave of a word, Sir Charles Pomander. Would you confound black and white because both are colours? Actress! Can you not see that she is a being like her fellows in nothing but a name? Her voice is truth, told by music: theirs are jingling instruments of falsehood

Pom. No—they are all instruments; but hers is more skilfully tuned and played upon.

Vane. She is a fountain of true feeling.

Pom. No—a pipe that conveys it, without spilling or retaining a drop.

Vane. She has a heart alive to every emotion.

Pom. And influenced by none.

Vane. She is a divinity to worship.

Pom. And a woman to fight shy of. No—no—we all know Peg Woffington; she is a decent actress on the boards, and a great actress off them. But I will tell you how to add a novel charm to her. Make her blush—ask her for the list of your predecessors.

Vane. (*With a mortified air.*) Sir Charles Pomander! But you yourself profess to admire her.

Pom. And so I do, hugely. Notwithstanding the charms of the mysterious Hebe I told you of, whose antediluvian coach I extricated from the Slough of Despond, near Barnet, on my way to town yesterday, I gave La Woffington a proof of my devotion only two hours ago.

Vane. How?

Pom. By offering her three hundred a year—house—coach—pin-money—my heart—and the et ceteras.

Vane. You? But she has refused.

Pom. My dear Arcadian, I am here to receive her answer. (VANE *crosses to* L. H.) You had better wait for it before making your avowal.

Vane. That avowal is made already; but I will wait, if but to see what a lesson the calumniated actress can read to the fine gentleman. *Exit* L. H.

Pom. The lesson will be set by me—Woffington will learn it immediately. It is so simple, only three words, £'s. s. d.
Exit D. H.

Trip. (*Speaking outside.*) Mr. Rich not in the theatre? Well, my engagements will allow of my waiting for a few minutes. (*Enter* TRIPLET *and* CALL-BOY L. TRIPLET *has a picture wrapped in baize and without a frame.*) And if you will just let me know when Mr. Rich arrives. (*Winks—touches his pocket.*) Heaven forgive me for raising groundless expectations!

Call-Boy. What name, sir?

Trip. Mr. Triplet.

Call-Boy. Triplet! there is something left for you in the hall, sir.   *Exit* CALL-BOY L.

Trip. I knew it. I sent him three tragedies. They are accepted; and he has left me a note in the hall, to fix the reading — at last. I felt it must come, soon or late; and it has come — late. Master of three arts, painting, writing, and acting, by each of which men grow fat, how was it possible I should go on perpetually starving. But that is all over now. My tragedies will be acted, the town will have an intellectual treat, and my wife and children will stab my heart no more with their hungry looks.

Enter CALL-BOY *with parcel* L.

Call-Boy. Here is the parcel for you, sir.

                                          Exit CALL-BOY L.

Trip. (*Weighs it in his hand.*) Why, how is this? Oh, I see; he returns them for some trifling alterations. Well, if they are judicious, I shall certainly adopt them, for (*opening the parcel*) managers are practical men. My tragedies! — Eh? here are but two! one is accepted! — no! they are all here (*sighs.*) Well, (*spitefully*) it is a thousand pounds out of Mr. Rich's pocket! poor man! I pity him; and my hungry mouths at home! Heaven knows where I am to find bread for them to-morrow! Everything that will raise a shilling I have sold or pawned. Even my poor picture here, the portrait of Mrs. Woffington from memory— I tried to sell that this morning at every dealer's in Long Acre — and not one would make me an offer.

Enter WOFFINGTON L. *reciting from a part.*

Woff.   " Now by the joys

Which my soul still has uncontroll'd pursued,

I would not turn aside from my least pleasure,

Though all thy force were armed to bar my way."

Trip. (*Aside,* R.) Mrs. Woffington, the great original of my picture!

Woff. (L.) "But like the birds, great nature's happy commoners,

Rifle the sweets"—I beg your pardon, sir!

Trip. Nay, madam, pray continue; happy the hearer and still happier the author of verses so spoken.

Woff. Yes, if you could persuade the authors how much they owe us, and how hard it is to find good music for indifferent words. Are you an author, sir?

Trip. In a small way, madam; I have here three tragedies.

Woff. (*Looking down at them with comical horror.*) Fifteen acts, mercy on us!

Trip. Which if I could submit to Mrs. Woffington's judgment —

Woff. (*Recoiling.*) ' I am no judge of such things, sir.

Trip. No more is the manager of this theatre.

Woff. What! has he accepted them?

Trip. No! madam! he has had them six months and returned them without a word.

Woff. Patience my good sir, patience! authors of tragedies should learn that virtue of their audiences. Do you know I called on Mr. Rich fifteen times before I could see him?

Trip. You, madam, impossible!

Woff. Oh, it was some years ago — and he has had to pay a hundred pounds for each of those little visits — let me see, — fifteen times — you must write twelve more tragedies — sixty acts — and then he will read one, and give you his judgment at last, and when you have got it — it won't be worth a farthing. (*Turns up reading her part.*)

Trip. (*Aside.*) One word from this laughing lady, and all my plays would be read — but I dare not ask her — she is up in the world, I am down. She is great — I am nobody — besides they say she is all brains and no heart. (*Crosses to* L. *Moves sorrowfully towards* L. D., *taking his picture.*)

Woff. He looks like a fifth act of a domestic tragedy. Stop, surely I know that doleful face — Sir !

Trip. Madam !

Woff. (*Beckons.*) We have met before ; — don't speak ; yours is a face that has been kind to me, and I never forget those faces.

Trip. Me, madam ! I know better what is due to you than to be kind to you.

Woff. To be sure ! it is Mr. Triplet, good Mr. Triplet of Goodman's Fields theatre.

Trip. It is, madam ; (*opening his eyes with astonishment*) but we don't call him Mr. nor even good.

Woff. Yes ; it is Mr. Triplet. (*Shakes both his hands warmly ; he timidly drops a tragedy or two.*) Don't you remember a little orange girl at Goodman's Fields you used sometimes to pat on the head and give sixpence to, some seven years ago, Mr. Triplet ?

Trip. Ha ! ha ! I do remember one, with such a merry laugh and bright eye ; and the broadest brogue of the whole sisterhood.

Woff. Get along with your blarney then, Mr. Triplet, an' is it the comether ye'd be puttin' on poor little Peggy ?

Trip. Oh ! oh ! gracious goodness, oh !

Woff. Yes ; that friendless orange girl was Margaret Woffington ! We'l, old friend, you see time has treated me well. I hope he has been as kind to you ; tell me Mr. Triplet.

Trip. (*Aside.*) I must put the best face on it with her. Yes, madam, he has blessed me with an excellent wife and three charming chil'ren. Mrs. Triplet was Mrs. Chatterton, of Goodman's Fields — great in the juvenile parts — you remember her ?

Woff. (*Very drily.*) Yes, I remember her ; where is she acting ?

Trip. Why, the cares of our family — and then her health. (*Sighs.*) She has not acted these eight months.

Woff. Ah ! — and are you still painting scenes ?

Trip. With the pen, madam, not the brush ! As the wag said, I have transferred the distemper from my canvas to my imagination, ha ! ha !

Woff. (*Aside.*) This man is acting gaiety. And have you pieces been successful ?

Trip Eminently so — in the closet; the managers have as yet excluded them from the stage.

Woff. Ah! now if those things were comedies, I would offer to act in one of them, and then the stage door would fly open at sight of the author.

Trip. I'll go home and write a comedy. (*Moves.*)

Woff. On second thoughts, perhaps you had better leave the tragedies with me.

Trip. My dear madam! — and you will read them?

Woff. Ahem! I will make poor Rich read them.

Trip. But he has rejected them.

Woff. That is the first step — reading comes after, when it comes at all.

Trip. (*Aside.*) I must fly home and tell my wife.

Woff. (*Aside.*) In the mean time I can put five guineas into his pocket. Mr. Triplet, do you write congratulatory verses — odes — and that sort of thing?

Trip. Anything, madam, from an acrostic to an epic.

Woff. Good, then I have a commission for you; I dine to-day at Mr. Vane's, in Bloomsbury Square. We shall want some verses. Will you oblige us with a copy?

Trip. (*Aside.*) A guinea in my way, at least. Oh, madam, do but give me a subject.

. *Woff.* Let's see — myself, if you can write on such a theme.

Trip. 'Tis the one I would have chosen out of all the heathen mythology; the praises of Venus and the Graces. I will set about it at once. (*Takes up portrait.*)

Woff. (*Sees picture.*) But what have you there? not another tragedy?

Trip. (*Blushing.*) A poor thing, madam, a portrait — my own painting from memory.

Woff. Oh! oh! I'm a judge of painted faces; let me see it.

Trip. Nay, madam!

Woff. I insist! (*She takes off the baize.*) My own portrait, as I live! and a good likeness too, or my glass flatters me like the rest of them. And this you painted from memory?

Trip. Yes, madam; I have a free admission to every part of the theatre before the curtain I have so enjoyed your acting, that

2

I have carried your face home with me every night, forgive my presumption, and tried to fix in the studio the impression of the stage.

Woff. Do you know your portrait has merit? I will give you a sitting for the last touches.

Trip. Oh, madam!

Woff. And bring all the critics — there, no thanks or I'll stay away. Stay, I must have your address.

Trip. (*Returning to her.*) On the fly leaf of each work, madam, you will find the address of James Triplet, painter, actor, and dramatic author, and Mrs. Woffington's humble and devoted servant. (*Bows ridiculously low, moves away, but returns with an attempt at a jaunty manner.*) Madam, you have inspired a son of Thespis with dreams of eloquence; you have tuned to a higher key a poet's lyre; you have tinged a painter's existence with brighter colors; and — and — (*gazes on her and tries in vain to speak*) God in heaven bless you, Mrs. Woffington!

(*Exit L. hastily.*)

Woff. So! I must look into this!

Enter SIR CHARLES POMANDER L.

Pom. Ah, Mrs. Woffington, I have just parted with an adorer of yours.

Woff. I wish I could part with them all.

Pom. Nay, this is a most original admirer, Ernest Vane, that pastoral youth who means to win La Woffington by agricultural courtship, who wants to take the star from its firmament, and stick it in a cottage.

Woff. And what does the man think I am to do without this (*imitates applause*) from my dear public's thousand hands.

Pom. You are to have that from a single mouth instead. (*Mimic a kiss.*)

Woff. Go on, tell me what more he says.

Pom. Why, he —

Woff. No, you are not to invent; I should detect your work in a minute, and you would only spoil this man.

Pom. He proposes to be your friend, rather than your lover; to fight for your reputation instead of adding to your eclat.

Woff. Oh! and is Mr. Vane your friend?

Pom. He is!

Woff. (*With significance.*) Why don't you tell him my real character, and send him into the country again!

Pom. I do; but he snaps his fingers at me and common sense and the world:—there is no getting rid of him, except in one way. I had this morning the honor, madam, of laying certain proposi-tions at your feet.

Woff. Oh, yes, your letter, Sir Charles. (*Takes it out of her pocket.*) I ran my eye down it as I came along, let me see—(*letter*)—"a coach," "a country house," "pin-money." Heigh ho! And I am *so* tired of houses, and coaches, and pins. Oh, yes, here is something. What is this you offer me, up in this corner? (*They inspect the letter together.*)

Pom. That,—my "heart!"

Woff. And you can't even write it; it looks just like "earth." There is your letter, Sir Charles. (*Curtseys and returns it; he takes it and bows.*)

Pom. Favor me with your answer.

Woff. You have it.

Pom. (*Laughing.*) Tell me, do you really refuse?

Woff. (*Inspecting him.*) Acting surprise? no, genuine! My good soul, are you so ignorant of the stage and the world, as not to know that I refuse such offers as yours every week of my life? I have refused so many of them, that I assure you I have begun to forget they are insults.

Pom. Insults, madam! They are the highest compliment you have left it in our power to pay you.

Woff. Indeed! Oh, I take your meaning. To be your mis-tress could be but a temporary disgrace; to be your wife might be a lasting discredit. Now, sir, having played your rival's game—

Pom. Ah!

Woff. And exposed your own hand, do something to recover the reputation of a man of the world. Leave the field before Mr. Vane can enjoy your discomfiture, for here he comes.

Pom. I leave you, madam, but remember, my discomfiture is neither your triumph nor your swain's. (*Exit* L.)

Woff I do enjoy putting down these irresistibles.

Enter VANE L.

At last! I have been here so long.

Vane. Alone ?

Woff. In company and solitude. What has annoyed you ?

Vane. Nothing.

Woff. Never try to conceal anything from me, I know the map of your face. These fourteen days you have been subject to some adverse influence ; and to-day I have discovered whose it is.

Vane. No influence can ever shake yours.

Woff. Dear friend, for your own sake, not mine ; trust your heart, eyes, and judgment.

Vane. I do. I love you ; your face is the shrine of sincerity, truth, and candor. I alone know you : your flatterers do not — your detractors — oh ! curse them !

Woff. You see what men are! Have I done ill to hide the riches of my heart from the heartless, and keep them all for one honest man, who will be my friend, I hope, as well as my lover ?

Vane. Ah, that is my ambition.

Woff. We actresses make good the old proverb, " Many lovers, but few friends." And oh ! it is we who need a friend. Will you be mine ?

Vane. I will. Then tell me the way for me, unequal in wit and address to many of your admirers, to win your esteem.

Woff. I will tell you a sure way ; never act in my presence, never try to be very clever or eloquent. Remember I am the goddess of tricks : I can only love my superior. Be honest and frank as the day, and you will be my superior ; and I shall love you, and bless the hour you shone on my artificial life.

Vane. Oh ! thanks, thanks, for this, I trust, is in my power !

Woff. Mind — it is no easy task : to be my friend is to respect me, that I may respect myself the more ; to be my friend is to come between me and the temptations of an unprotected life — the recklessness of a vacant heart.

Vane. I will place all that is good about me at your feet. I will sympathise with you when you are sad ; I will rejoice when you are gay.

Woff. Will you scold me when I do wrong ?

Vane. Scold you?

Woff. Nobody scolds me now — a sure sign nobody loves me. Will you scold me?

Vane. (*Tenderly.*) I will try! and I will be loyal and frank. You will not hate me for a confession I make myself? (*Agitated.*)

Woff. I shall like you better — oh! so much better.

Vane. Then I will own to you —

Woff. Oh! do not tell me you have loved others before me; I could not bear to hear it.

Vane. No — no — I never *loved* till now.

Woff. Let me hear that only. I am jealous even of the past. Say you never loved but me — never mind whether it is true — say so; — but it is true, for you do not yet know love. Ernest, shall I make you love me, as none of your sex ever loved? with heart, and brain, and breath, and life, and soul?

Vane. Teach me so to love, and I am yours for ever. (*Pause.*) And now you will keep your promise, to make me happy with your presence this morning at the little festival I had arranged with Cibber and some of our friends of the theatre.

Woff. I shall have so much pleasure; but *apropos*, you must include Snarl and Soaper in your list.

Vane. What! the redoubtable Aristarchuses of the pit?

Woff. Yes. Oh, you don't know the consequences of loving an actress. You will have to espouse my quarrels, manage my managers, and invite my critics to dinner.

Vane. They shall be invited, never fear.

Woff. And I've a trust for you; poor Triplet's three tragedies. If they are as heavy in the hearing as the carrying — but here comes your rival, poor Pomander. (*Crosses to* L.)

Enter SIR CHARLES L.

You will join our party at Mr. Vane's, Sir Charles? You promised, you know. (*Crosses to* L.)

Pom. (*Coldly.*) *Desole* to forfeit such felicity; but I have business.

Vane. (*As he passes, crosses to* C.) By-the-bye, Pomander, that answer to your letter to Mrs. Woffington?

2*

Woff. He has received it. *N'est ce pas*, Sir Charles ? You see how radiant it has made him ! Ha ! ha !

(Exeunt WOFFINGTON and VANE L. II.)

Pom. Laughing devil ! If you had wit to read beneath men's surface, you would know it is no jest to make an enemy of Sir Charles Pomander.

Enter HUNDSDON R.

Hunds. Servant, Sir Charles.

Pom. Ah, my yeoman pricker, with news of the mysterious Hebe of my Barnet rencontre. Well, sirrah, you stayed by the coach as I bade you ?

Hunds. Yes, Sir Charles.

Pom. And pumped the servants ?

Hunds. Yes, Sir Charles, till they swore they'd pump on me.

Pom. My good fellow, contrive to answer my questions without punning, will you ?

Hunds. Yes, Sir Charles.

Pom. What did you learn from them ? Who is the lady, their mistress ?

Hunds. She is on her way to town to join her husband. They have only been married a twelve-month ; and he has been absent from her half the time.

Pom. Good. Her name ?

Hunds. Vane.

Pom. Vane !

Hunds. Wife of Mr. Ernest Vane, a gentleman of good estate, Willoughby Manor, Huntingdonshire.

Pom. What ! — What ! — His wife, by heaven ! Oh ! here is rare revenge. Ride back, sirrah, and follow the coach to its destination.

Hunds. They took master for a highwayman If they knew him as well as I do, they wouldn't do the road such an injustice.

(Exit R.)

Pom. (*With energy.*) I'll after them ; and if I can but manage that Vane shall remain ignorant of her arrival, I may confront Hebe with Thalia ; introduce the wife to the mistress under the husband's roof. Aha! my Arcadian pair, there may be a guest at your banquet you little expect, besides Sir Charles Pomander!

(*Exit* L.)

SCENE II. 4 *and* 6 G. — *A spacious and elegant Apartment in the House of* MR. VANE, *with* C. *doors opening into a Garden formally planted, with Statues, &c. Set door* 2 E. R. H. *Set door* 3 E. L. H. *A table set for a collation, with Fruits, Flowers, Wine, and Plate in* C. *Settees and high-backed Chairs, a Side Table with Plate, Salvers, &c. on* R. H.

COLANDER *discovered arranging table.*

Col. So! malmsey, fruit, tea, coffee, yes! all is ready against their leaving the dining-room!

Enter JAMES BURDOCK, *a salver with letters in his hand,* 1 E. L.

Bur. Post letters, Master Colander.

Col. Put 'em on the salver. (*Burdock does so.*) You may go, honest Burdock. (*Burdock fidgets, turning the letters on the salver.*) When I say you *may* go — that means you *must*; the stable is your place when the family is not in Huntingdonshire, and at present the family is in London.

Bur. And I wish it was in Huntingdonshire, with the best part of it, and that's mistress. Poor thing! A twelvemonth married, and six months of it as good as a widow.

Col. We write to her, James, and receive her replies.

Bur Aye! but we don't read 'em, it seems.

Col. We intend to do so at our leisure — meanwhile we make ourselves happy among the wits and the players.

Bur. And she do make others happy among the poor and the suffering.

Col. James Burdock, property has its duties, as well as its rights. Master enjoys the rights in town, and mistress discharges the duties in the country; 'tis the division of labor — and now vanish, honest James, the company will be here directly, and you know master can't abide the smell of the stable. (*Crosses to* L.)

Bur. But, Master Colander, do let him have this letter from missus. (*Holds out the letter he has taken from the salver.*)

Col. James Burdock, you are incorrigible. Have I not given it to him once already? and didn't he fling it in my face and call me a puppy? I respect Mistress Vane, James; but I must remember what's due to myself—I shan't take it.

(*Exit* COLANDER, 3 E. L.)

Bur. Then I will—there! Poor dear lady! I can't abear that her letters, with her heart in 'em, I'll be sworn, should lie unopened. Barnet post mark!—why, how can that be? Well, its not my business. (*Puts salver on table* 2 E. L.) Master shall have it though. (*Hurried knocking heard.*) There goes that door, ah! I thought it wouldn't be quiet long—what a rake-helly place this London is! (*Exit* L.)

Re-enter with MRS. VANE *in a hood and travelling dress,* 1 E. L.

Bur. Stop! stop! I don't think master can see you, young woman.

Mabel. Why, James Burdock, have you forgotten your mistress? (*Removes her hood.*)

Bur. Mistress! Why Miss Mabel—I ask your pardon, miss—I mean, madam. Bless your sweet face!—here, John, Thomas!

Mabel. Hush!

Bur. Lord, lord! come at last! oh! how woundy glad I am, to be sure—oh! lord, lord, my old head's all of a muddle with joy to see your kind face again.

Mabel. (R.) But Ernest—Mr. Vane, James. is he well—and happy—and (*sees his change of face*)—eh! he is well, James?

Bur. Yes, yes, quite well, and main happy.

Mabel. And is he very impatient to see me?

Bur. (*Aside.*) Lord help her!

Mabel. But mind, James, not a word; he doesn't expect me till six, and 'tis now scarce four. Oh! I shall startle him so!

Bur. Yes, yes, madam; you'll startle him woundily.

Mabel. Oh! it will be so delightful to pop out upon him un-awares — will it not, James ?

Bur. Yes, Miss Mabel, — that is, madam ; but hadn't I better prepare him like ?

Mabel. Not for the world. You know, James, when one is wishing for any one very much, the last hour's waiting is always the most intolerable, so when he is most longing to see me, and counting the minutes to six, I'll just open the door, and steal be-hind him, and fling my arms round his neck, and — but I shall be caught if I stay prattling here, and I must brush the dust from my hair, and smooth my dress, or I shall not be fit to be seen ; so not a word to anybody, James, I insist, or I shall be angry. Where is my room ? (*Goes to* 2 E. R. *and opens door*) Oh, here !

Bur. Your room, Miss Mabel ; no ! no ! that is Mr. Vane's room, Ma'am.

Mabel. Well, Mr. Vane's room is my room, I suppose. (*Paus-ing at door.*) He is not there, is he ?

Bur. No, ma'am, he is in the dining-room. (*Knock.*) Anon ! anon !

Mabel. I fear my trunks will not be here in time for me to dress ; but Ernest will not mind. He will see my heart in my face, and forgive my travelling sacque. (*Exit into apartment* R. 2 E.)

Bur. Poor thing ! poor thing ! (*Knock* L.) There goes that door again — darn me if I go till I've seen Colander. Anon, Miss Mabel ! (*Going to door* 2 E. R.)

HUNDSDON *enters* 3 E. L.

Hunds. (*Aside and looking at Burdock.*) For all the world the twin brother to those bumpkins behind Hebe's coach. Well, my honest fellow !

Bur. Well, my jack-a-dandy !

Hunds. Can'st bring me Sir Charles Pomander hither, my honest fellow ?

Bur. Here he's bringing himself, my jack-a-dandy.

(*Exit* C. L.)

Hunds. For so pretty a creature, she hath an establishment of the veriest brutes. Ah ! here comes Master !

Enter SIR CHARLES POMANDER 3 E. L.

Pom. Well! is she arrived?

Hunds. (*Aside to* POMANDER.) I've marked her down, sir. Sh
is here — in that room. (*Pointing* 2 E. R. II.)

Pom. Is her arrival known?

Hunds. But to a rustic savage of a servant.

Pom. Good! Take thy sheep's face out of sight, incontinently.

Hunds. Yes, Sir Charles.

Pom. Hold! I have kept thee sober for two days. Here's for
thee to make a beast of thyself.

Hunds. Nay, I'll disappoint him, and profit by sobriety.

                                        (*Exit* 1 E. L.)

Pom. So, the train is laid and I hold the match in my hand.
(COLANDER *returns with servants, who bring tea, coffee, &c.*)

Enter VANE, WOFFINGTON, QUIN, CLIVE, CIBBER, SNARL
    and SOAPER, *as from the dining-room, laughing,* C. D.

Quin. I hate this detestable innovation of outlandish drawing
room drinks — your tea and coffee — pshaw!

Vane. But you forget the ladies, Mr. Quin, and in the presence
of Mr. Cibber too, whom I cannot thank enough for the honor of
this visit.

Cib. Nay, Sir, I bring my wit in exchange for your wine; we
barter our respective superfluities.

Quin. Good wine is no superfluity, Mr. Cibber; 'tis a necessary
of life, just as much as good victuals.

Soap. I vow Mr. Cibber is as lively as ever, and doesn't look
a day older: does he Mr. Snarl?

Snarl. 'Tis that there's no room on Mr. Cibber's face for
another wrinkle.

Cib. (*Takes snuff.*) Puppies!

Quin. Really this is too bad, the coffee is getting cold. (*Goes
to the table,* R.)

Clive. So, no wonder Quin is getting warm. (*Gives him coffee.*
Here, bear! (WOFFINGTON *presides over tea.*)

Cib. You have a charming house here, Mr. Vane, I know it is poor dear Lord Loungeville's time. You may just remember him, Sir Charles ?

Pom. I never read ancient history.

Cib. Puppy ! An unrivalled gallant, Peggy. Oh, the *petits soupers* we have had here ! Loungeville was a great creature, Sir Charles. I wish you may ever be like him.

Pom. I sincerely trust not. (*Goes to table* c.) I do not feel at all anxious to figure in the museum of town antiquities — labelled, " Old Beau, very curious."

Cib. (*Aside.*) Coxcomb ! Let me tell you your old beaux were the only ones worthy of winging the shafts from Cupid's quiver.

Snarl. Witness Mr. Cibber. (*Goes to table* c.)

Woff. Oh, Colley is like old port — the more ancient he grows the more exquisite his perfume becomes.

Soap. Capital ! She alludes to Mr. Cibber's pulvilio.

Snarl. And the crustier he gets.

Soap. Delicious ! He alludes to Mr. Cibber's little irritability.

Cib. Ah, laugh at us old fellows as you will, young people ; but I have known Loungeville entertain a fine lady in this very saloon, whilst a rival was fretting and fuming on the other side of that door. Ha, ha ! (*Sighs.*) It is all over now.

Pom. Nay, Mr. Cibber, why assume that the house has lost its virtue in our friend's hands ?

Cib. Because, young gentleman, you all want *sçavoir faire ;* the fellows of the day are all either unprincipled heathens like you, or cold blooded Amadisses like our host. The true *Preux des Dames,* (*regretfully*) went out with the full periwig, stap my vitals !

Quin. A bit of toast, Mr. Cibber ? (*Goes to table.*)

Cib. Jemmy, you are a brute.

Quin. You refuse, sir ?

Cib. (*With dignity.*) No, sir, I accept. (Quin *takes plate of toast to table,* R.)

Pom. (*Goes to table.*) You Antediluvians must not flatter yourselves you have monopolized iniquity, or that the deluge washed away intrigue, and that a rake is a fossil. We are still as vicious as you could desire, Mr. Cibber. What if I bet a cool hundred round that Vane has a petticoat in the next room, and Mrs. Woffington shall bring her out.

Vane. Pomander! (*Checks himself.*) But we all know Pomander.

Pom. Not yet, *but you shall.* Now don't look so abominably in-
nocent, my dear fellow, I ran her to earth in this house not ten
minutes ago.

Cib. Have her out, Peggy! I know the run — there's the
cover — Hark forward! Yoicks! Ha, ha, ha! (*Coughing.*) Ho,
ho!

Vane. Mr. Cibber, age and infirmity are privileged but for you,
Sir Charles Pomander —

Woff. Don't be angry. Do you not see it is a jest, and, as
might be expected, a sorry one?

Vane. A jest; it must go no farther, or by Heaven! — (Woffington *places her hand on his shoulder* — Mabel *appears* D. R.
2 E.)

Mabel. Ernest, dear Ernest! (Woffington *removes her hand
quickly.*)

Vane. Mabel!

Pom. I win. (*A pause of silent amazement.* Vane *looks round
on the reverse side of* Woffington.)

Woff. (*Aside to* Vane.) Who is this?

Vane. My — my wife! (*All rise and bow.* Colander *places
chair for* Mrs Vane.)

Cib. 'Fore Gad! he is stronger than Loungeville.

Mabel. You are not angry with me for this silly trick? After
all I am but two hours before my time. You know, dearest, I
said six in my letter.

Vane. Yes — yes!

Mabel. And you have had three days to prepare you, for I
wrote like a good wife to ask leave before starting, ladies and gentlemen; but he never so much as answered my letter, madam.
(*To* Woffington, *who winces.*)

Vane. Why, you c — c — couldn't doubt, Mabel? (Cibber
joins Snarl *and* Soaper *at table* L.)

Mabel. No, silence gives consent; but I beg your pardon, ladies,
(*looking to* Woffington,) for being so glad to see my husband.

Snarl. 'Tis a failing, madam, you will soon get over in town.
(*Laugh.*)

Mabel. Nay, sir, I hope not; but I warrant me you did not look for me so soon.

Woff. Some of us did not look for you at all.

Mabel. What! Ernest did not tell you he expected me?

Woff No; he told us the entertainment was in honor of a lady's first visit to his house; but he did *not* tell us that lady was his wife.

Vane. (*Aside to* WOFF.) Spare her!

Woff. (*Aside to* VANE.) Have you spared me?

Pom. No doubt he wished to procure us that agreeable surprise, which you have procured him.

Snarl. And which he evidently enjoys so much.

Soap. Oh, evidently. (CIBBER, SNARL *and* SOAPER *laugh, aside.*)

Vane. You had better retire, Mabel, and change your travelling dress.

Mabel. Nay; you forget, I am a stranger to your friends. Will you not introduce me to them first?

Vane. No, no; it is not usual to introduce in the polite world.

Woff. We always introduce ourselves. (*Rises. All come down except* VANE *and* QUIN.)

Vane. (*Aside to* WOFF.) Madam, for pity's sake!

Woff. So, if you will permit me.

Pom. (*Aside.*) Now for the explosion!

Vane. (*Aside.*) She will shew me no mercy.

Woff. (*Introducing* CLIVE.) Lady Lurewell!

Clive. Madam! (*She curtsies.*) If she had made me a commoner, I'd have exposed her on the spot.

Woff. (*Introducing him.*) Sir John Brute!

Quin. (*She comes forward, aside to* WOFF.) Hang it! Falstaff!

Woff. Sir John Brute Falstaff! we call him for brevity, Brute.

Pom. (*Aside.*) Missed fire! Confound her ready wit.

Vane. (*Aside.*) I breathe again.

Woff. That is Lord Foppington, (*crosses to* CIBBER,) a butterfly of long standing and a little gouty. Sir Charles Pomander!

Pom. Who will spare you the trouble of a description, (*crossing to* MABEL,) as he has already had the honor of avowing himself Mrs. Vane's most humble servant.

3

Vane. How ! (*Advances* c.)

Mabel. The good gentleman who helped my coach out of the slough yesterday.

Vane. Ah ! (*Goes up to the table* L. U. E.)

Woff. Mr. Soaper, Mr. Snarl — gentlemen who would butter and cut up their own fathers !

Mabel. Bless me ; cannibals !

Woff. (*With a sweet smile.*) No ; critics.

Mabel. But yourself, madam ?

Woff. (*Curtseying.*) I am the Lady Betty Modish, at your service.

Clive. (*Aside to* QUIN.) And anybody else's.

Mabel. Oh dear, so many lords and ladies !

Vane. Pray go, and change your dress, Mabel.

Mabel. What ! before you hear the news of dear Willoughby, Ernest ? Lady Betty, I had so many things to tell him, and he sends me away.

Cibber. Nay, really, 'tis too cruel.

Woff. Pray, madam, your budget of country news ; clotted cream so seldom comes to London quite fresh.

Mabel. There you see, Ernest. First, then, Grey Gillian is turned out for a brood mare, so old George won't let me ride her.

Woff. The barbarian !

Mabel. Old servants are such hard masters, my lady ; and my Barbary hen has laid two eggs, Ernest. Heaven knows the trouble we have had to bring her to it. And dame Best (that's his old nurse, Lady Lurewell) has had soup and pudding from the hall every day.

Quin. Soup and pudding ! that's what I call true charity.

Mabel. Yes ; and once she went so far as to say, "it wasn't altogether a bad pudding." I made it with these hands.

Cibber. Happy pudding !

Vane. Is this mockery, sir ?

Cibber. No, sir, it is gallantry ; an exercise that died before you were born. Madam, shall I have the honor of kissing one of the fair hands that made that most favored of puddings ?

Mabel. Oh, my lord, you may, because you are so old ; but I don't say so for a young gentleman, unless it was Ernest himself, and he doesn't ask me. (CIBBER, SNARL *and* SOAPER *go up.*)

Vane. (*Angrily.*) My dear Mabel, pray remember we are not at Willoughby.

Clive. Now, bear, where's your paw ? (*Going up* R.)

Quin. All I regret is, that I go without having helped Mrs Vane to buttered toast.

Clive. Poor Quin, first to quit his bottle half finished, and now, to leave the run of the table for a walk in the garden !

(*Exeunt* C. D. L.)

Vane. Let me shew you to your apartment. (*Rings bell, leads her to door* R.)

Enter SERVANT L. H.

Bid the musicians play. (*Exit* SERVANT L. H.)

(VANE *offers his arm to* WOFFINGTON.) Let me conduct you to the garden.

(*Music without* U. E. R. H. WOFFINGTON *gives her hand and goes off with* VANE L. C. — *in going out she looks back. Music heard.*)

Woff. (*Aside.*) Yes ; there are triumphs out of the Theatre.

(*Exit with* VANE L. C.)

Cibber. (*Crosses to* MABEL.) Mr. Vane's garden will lack its fairest flower, madam, if you desert us.

Mabel. (R.) Nay, my lord, there are fairer here than I.

Pom. (*Goes up to* C. L.) Jealous, I see, already. Shall I tell her all ? No ; I will let the green-eyed monster breach the fortress, and then I shall walk in without a contest.

Cibber. (*Meeting* SIR CHARLES *at* C. L.) Your arm, sir Charles.

Pom. At your service, Mr. Cibber.

(*Exeunt* POMANDER *and* CIBBER C. D. L.)

Snarl. A pleasant party, Mr. Soaper.

Soap. Remarkably. Such a delightful meeting of husband and wife, Mr. Snarl ! (*Exeunt* C. D. L. H. *Music ceases.*)

Mabel. How kind they all are to me, except him whose kindness alone I value, and he must take Lady Betty's hand instead of mine ; but that is good breeding I suppose. I wish there was no such thing as good breeding in London, any more than in Huntingdonshire.

Col. (*Without, angrily,* C. L.) I tell you Mr. Vane is not at home.

Mabel. What is the matter?

(TRIPLET *discovered attempting to force his way through* C. D. L. H. COLANDER *bars his entrance.* TRIPLET *carries a portfolio, two volumes, and a roll of manuscript.*)

Col. I tell you he is not at home, sir.

Mabel. How can you say so, when you know he is in the garden.

Col. Ugh! (*Aside.*) The simpleton.

Mabel. Show the gentleman in.

Col. Gentleman!

Trip. A thousand thanks, madam, for this condescension; I will wait Mr. Vane's leisure in the hall.

Mabel. Nay, sir, not in the hall, 'tis cold there. Tell Mr. Vane the gentleman waits. Will you go, sirrah?

Col. I am gone, madam. (*Aside.*) Porter to players! and now usher to an author! curse me if I stand it.

(*Exit* C. D. L. H.)

Trip. (*Advancing.*) A thousand apologies, madam, for the trouble I put you to. I — madam — you overwhelm me with confusion.

Mabel. Nay — nay — be seated.

Trip. Madam, you are too condescending. (*Aside.*) Who can she be? (*Bows again and again.*)

Mabel. Nay, sit down and rest you. (TRIPLET *bows, and sits on the edge of a chair, with astonishment.*) You look sadly adust and tired.

Trip. Why, yes, madam; it is a long way from Lambeth; and the heat is surpassing. (*Takes his handkerchief out to wipe his brow; returns it somewhat hastily to his pocket.*) I beg your pardon, I forgot myself.

Mabel. (*Aside.*) Poor man, he looks sadly lean and hungry. And I'll be bound you came in such a hurry, you forget — you mustn't be angry with me — to have your dinner first.

Trip. How strange! madam, you have guessed it. I did forget — he, he! — I have such a head — not that I need have forgotten it — but being used to forget it, I did not remember not to forget it to-day. (*Smiles absurdly.*)

Mabel. (*Pours wine.*) A glass of wine, sir ?

Trip. (*Rising and bowing.*) Nay, madam. (*Eyes the wine — drinks.*) Nectar, as I am a man. (*She helps him to refreshments.*)

Mabel. Take a biscuit, sir ?

Trip. (*Eating.*) Madam, as I said before, you overwhelm me. Walking certainly makes one hungry. (*Eats.*) Oh, yes, it certainly does ; (MABEL *helps him*) and though I do not usually eat at this time of the day. (MABEL *helps him again.*)

Mabel. I am sorry Mr. Vane keeps you waiting.

Trip. By no means, madam, it is very fortunate — (*Eats*) I mean it procures me the pleasure of (*eats*) your society. Besides, the servants of the Muse are used to waiting. What we are not used to is (*she fills his glass*) being waited on by Hebe and the Twelve Graces, whose health I have the honor ! — Falernian, as I'm a poet !

Mabel. A poet ! (*Clapping her hands.*) Oh, I am so glad ! I never thought to see a living poet ; I do so love poetry !

Trip. Ha ! it is in your face, madam. I should be proud to have your opinion of this trifle composed by me for Mr. Vane, in honor of the lady he expected this morning.

Mabel. (*Aside.*) Dear Ernest ! how ungrateful I was. Nay, sir, I think I know the lady ; and it would be hardly proper for me to hear them.

Trip. (*After placing the MS. by the side of his plate, with another plate to keep it open ; laying his hand on his heart.*) Oh, strictly correct, madam. James Triplet never stooped to the loose taste of the town, even in trifles of this sort. (*Reads.*) " When first from Albion's isle — "

Mabel. Take another glass of wine first.

Trip. Madam, I will. (*Drinks.*) I thank you infinitely. (*Reads.*) " When first from Albion's isle — "

Mabel. Another biscuit. (*Helps him.*)

Trip. Madam, (*eats a mouthful,*) you do me infinite honor. (*Reads again.*) " When first from Albion's isle — "

Mabel. No — no — no ! (*Stops her ears.*) Mr. Vane intended them for a surprise, and it would spoil his pleasure were I to hear them from you.

Trip. (*Sighs.*) As you please, madam ! But you would have

3*

liked them, for the theme inspired me. The kindest, the most
generous and gifted of women!—don't you agree with me,
madam?

Mabel. (*Laughs.*) No indeed!

Trip. Ah! if you knew her as I do.

Mabel. I ought to know her better, sir.

Trip. Her kindness to me, for instance: a poor devil like me,
if I may be allowed the expression.

Mabel. Nay, you exaggerate her trifling act of civility.

Trip. (*Reproachfully.*) Act of civility, madam! Why she has
saved me from despair—from starvation perhaps.

Mabel. (*Aside.*) Poor thing! how hungry he must have been.

Trip. And she's to sit to me for her portrait, too.

Mabel. Her portrait! (*Aside.*) Oh, another attention of
Ernest's—but I thought you were a poet, sir?

Trip. So I am, madam, from an epitaph to an epic. Let me
convince you. (*Reads.*) " When first from Albion's isle —"

Mabel. But you spoke just now of painting. Are you a
painter too?

Trip. From a scene to a sign-board; from a house-front to an
historical composition.

Mabel. Oh, what a clever man! And so Ernest commissioned
you to paint this portrait?

Trip. No; for that I am indebted to the lady herself.

Mabel. The lady? (*Rises.*)

Trip. I expected to find her here;—perhaps you can inform
me whether she is arrived?

Mabel. (*Aside.*) Not my portrait after all. Who?

Trip. Mrs. Woffington.

Mabel. Woffington? No, there was no such name among the
guests Mr. Vane received to-day.

Trip. That is strange! She was to be here; and therefore I
expedited the verses in her honor.

Mabel. (*Ruefully.*) In *her* honor?

Trip. Yes, madam; the subject is " Genius trampling on
Envy." It begins. (*Reads.*) " When first from Albion's isle —"

Mabel. Nay, I do not care to hear them, for I do not know the
lady.

Trip. Few really know her; but at least you have seen her act.

Mabel. Act! Is she an actress?

Trip. An actress, madam! *The* Actress!—and you have never seen her! Madam, you have a great pleasure before you; to see her act is a privilege, but to act with her, as I once did, though she doesn't remember it—I was hissed, madam, owing to circumstances which for the credit of our common nature I suppress.

Mabel. An actor too!

Trip. And it was in a farce of my own too, madam, which was damned—accidentally.

Mabel. And a play-writer?

Trip. Plays, madam! I have written a library of them; but the madmen who manage the patent houses won't act them and make their fortunes. You see in me a dramatic gold mine, lost because no company will work me.

Mabel. Yes, yes; but tell me! this actress:—Mr. Vane admires her?

Trip. Mr. Vane is a gentleman of taste, madam.

Mabel. And she was to have been here? There were none but persons of quality—ah! the news of my intended arrival—no doubt—well Mr. ——

Trip. Triplet, madam! James Triplet, 10, Hercules Buildings, Lambeth: occasional verses, odes, epithalamia, elegies, dedications, translations, and every species of literary composition executed with spirit, punctuality, and secrecy. Portraits painted, and lessons given in declamation and the dramatic art. The card, madam, (*presents card*) of him, who, to all these qualifications adds a prouder still—that of being your humble, devoted, and truly grateful servant—James Triplet. (*Bows and moves off—returns.*) The fact is, madam, it may appear strange to you, but a kind hand has not so often been held out to me, that I should forget it, especially when that hand is so fair and gracious as yours. May I be permitted, madam? (*Puts her hand to his lips.*) You will impute it to gratitude rather than audacity—madam, I am gone—I flatter myself, James Triplet, throughout this charming interview, has conducted himself like what he may not appear to be—a gentleman. Madam, I take my final leave. (*Exit* 1 E. L.)

Mabel.   Invite an actress to his house! but Ernest is so warm-hearted and generous; no doubt 'tis as Mr. Triplet says; he has admired her acting and wished to mark his sense of her merit by presenting her these verses, and a dinner. (*Music.*) These poor actors and actresses! I have seen some of them down in Huntingdonshire, and I know what a kindness it is to give them a good meal. (*Crosses to* L.)

Enter SIR CHARLES POMANDER L. C. *down* R.

Pom.   What, madam, all alone, here as in Huntingdonshire! Force of habit.   A husband with a wife in Huntingdonshire is so like a bachelor.

Mabel.   Sir!

Pom.   And our excellent Ernest is such a favorite.

Mabel.   No wonder.

Pom.   There are not many who can so pass in six months from the larva state of Bumpkin to the butterfly existence of Beau.   (*Music ceases.*)

Mabel.   Yes; (*sadly*) I find him changed.

Pom.   Changed? transformed! He is now the prop of the Cocoa-tree — the star of Ranelagh — the Lauzun of the Green Room.

Mabel.   The Green Room?

Pom.   Ah, I forgot! you are fresh from Eden; the Green Room, my dear madam, is the bower where fairies put off their wings and goddesses become dowdies — where Lady Macbeth weeps over her lap-dog's indigestion, and Belvidera groans over the amount of her last milliner's bill. In a word, the Green Room is the place where actors and actresses become mere men and women, and the name is no doubt derived from the general character of its unprofessional visitors.

Mabel.   And is it possible that Ernest, Mr. Vane, frequents such places?

Pom.   He has earned in six months a reputation that many a fine gentleman would give his ears for — not a scandalous journal he has not figured in — not an actress of reputation or no reputation, but gossip has given him for a conquest.

Mabel. You forget, sir, you are speaking to his wife.

Pom. On the contrary, madam ; but you would be sure to learn this, and it is best you should learn it at once and from a friend.

Mabel. Is it the office of a friend to calumniate the husband to the wife ?

Pom. When he admires the wife, he reprobates the husband's ill-taste in neglecting her.

Mabel. Do you suppose I did not know of his having invited Mrs. Woffington to his house to-day ?

Pom. What ! you found her out ? you detected the Actress-of-all-work under the airs of Lady Betty Modish.

Mabel. Lady Betty Modish !

Pom. Yes ; that was La Woffington.

Mabel. Whom he had invited hither to present her with a copy of verses.

Pom. Et cetera.

Mabel. And who in an actress' sudden frolic, gave herself and her companions those titles without my husband's connivance.

Pom. Vane could not have explained it half so well. These women are incredibles.

Mabel. Had the visit been in any other character, do you think he would have chosen for it the day of my arrival ?

Pom. Certainly not, if he knew you were coming.

Mabel. And he did know; why here (*seeing letters on table* L.) are my letters announcing my intention to start — my progress on the road — the last written from Barnet, only yesterday.

While speaking she has gone to the salver, on L. H. *and hastily taken the letters, which she offers* POMANDER *with triumph. He takes them with an uncertain air, looks at them — gives them back to her after a pause.*

Pom. (*Coolly.*) The seals have not been broken, madam.

Mabel. (*Bursting into tears.*) Unopened ! It is too true ! Flung aside unread ! and I have learned by heart every word he ever wrote to me. Sir, you have struck down the hope and trust of my life without remorse. May heaven forgive you !

Pom. Madam ! let me, who have learned to adore you —

Mabel. I may no longer hold a place in my husband's heart — but I am still mistress of his house — leave it, sir !

Pom. Your wishes are my law — (*going*) but here they come!
(*Crosses to* L.) Use the right of a wife, watch them unseen, and
you will soon learn whether I am mistaken, or you misinformed.

Mabel. (*Violently.*) No! I will not dog my husband's steps at
the bidding of his treacherous friend. (*Watches* POMANDER *out.*)

Pom. (*Aside.*) She will watch them.   (*Exit.*)

After a moment or two of irresolution, MABEL *crouches down behind
a chair. Enter* VANE C. L. *conducting* WOFFINGTON : *they pass
without observing* MABEL.

Vane. But one word — I can explain all. Let me accompany
you to this painter's. I am ready to renounce credit — character —
wife — all for you !

Woff. I go alone, sir. Call Mrs. Woffington's coach.

         Exit WOFFINGTON, *followed by* VANE. 1 E. L.

Mabel. (*Starting from seat.*) Oh, no, no ! — you cannot use me
so. Ernest ! Husband ! (*Tries to rush towards* L. D. *Swoons.*
VANE *returns.*)

Vane. Who called me ? Mabel — my wife ! (*Stamps.*) help,
here ! — what have I done ? (*He raises her in his arms.* **Quick
drop.**)

END OF ACT ONE.

ACT II.

SCENE I. 3. G. *A large roughly furnished Garret.* *Set door* 2
G. R. II. *Set door* 2 E. L. II. *Easel with Woffington's Picture on
it, half concealed by a green baize drapery. Colors, Palette,
Pencils, Maulstick, &c., &c. Mrs. Triplet reclining in a large
chair, and wrapped up like an invalid, on* R. II. *Violin hanging
against wall. Triplet seated at small Table writing,* C. *Two
Children. Wooden Chairs. Boy is rocking Cradle and singing.*

Trip. Do keep those children quiet, Jane.

Mrs. T. (*On* R.) Hush, my dears, let your father write his
comedy. Comedy seems so troublesome to write.

Trip. Yes! somehow sorrow comes more natural to me!
(*Pause.*) I've got a bright thought; you see, Jane, they are all
at a sumptuous banquet: all the Dramatis Personæ except the
poet, (*writes*) music — sparkling wine — massive plate — soups —
fish — shall I have three dishes of fish? venison — game — pickles
and provocatives in the centre, then up jumps one of the guests,
and says he —

Boy. Oh, dear! I am so hungry!

Girl. And so am I.

Trip. That is an absurd remark, Lysimachus, not four hours
after breakfast.

Boy. But father — there wasn't any breakfast for breakfast!

Trip. Now I ask you, Mrs. Triplet — how am I to write
comic scenes, if you let Lysimachus and Roxalana there put the
heavy business in every five minutes?

Mrs. T. Forgive them, the poor things *are* hungry!

Trip. Then they must learn to be hungry in another room.
They shan't cling around my pen and paralyze it, just when it is
going to make all our fortunes; (*rises*) but you women have no
consideration — send 'em all to bed, every man Jack of 'em.
(*Children raise a doleful cry.*) Hungry! hungry! Is that a pro-

per expression to use before a father who is sitting down, (*seats himself*) all gayety — and hilarity to write a Com — a Com — (*chokes.*) Where's the youngest — where's Cleopatra? (Mrs. T. *brings child to him — he takes her on his knee.*)

Girl. Father, I'm not so very hungry!

Boy. (*Who has come to his father.*) And I'm not hungry at all — I had a piece of bread and butter yesterday!

Trip. Wife; they'll drive me mad!

Boy. (*Sotto voce.*) Mother; father made us hungry out of his book.

Girl. Is it a cookery book, father?

Trip. Ha! ha! is my comedy a cookery book? The young rogues say more good things than I do — that is the worst of it. Wife, I took that sermon I wrote —

Mrs. T. And beautiful it was, James.

Trip. I took it to the Reverend Gentleman, and he would not have it, he said it was too hard upon sin for the present day. (*Dashes at the paper.*) Ah! if my friend Mrs. Woffington would but leave this stupid comedy and take to tragedy, things would smile again.

Mrs. T. Oh, James, how can you expect anything from that woman? You won't believe what all the world says — you measure folk by your own good heart.

Trip. I haven't a good heart, I spoke like a brute to you just now.

Mrs. T. Never mind, James, I wonder how you put up with me at all! a sick useless creature. I often wish to die, for your sake — I know you would do better — I am such a weight round your neck. (*Triplet takes Mrs. T. to chair — then returns with energy to his comedy — boy brings violin.*)

Boy. Play us a tune on the fiddle, father!

Mrs. T. Ay do, husband! that often helps you in your writing. (*Triplet plays a merry tune dolefully.*)

Trip. It won't do, music must be in the heart, or it will never come out of the fingers. (*Puts fiddle down — boy takes it and puts it in the cradle.*) No! let us be serious and finish the comedy — perhaps it hitches because I forgot to invoke Thalia — the Muse of Comedy, Mrs. Triplet; she must be a black-hearted jade if she won't lend a broad grin to a poor devil starving in the middle of his hungry little ones.

Mrs. T. Heathen goddesses can't help us. We had better pray to heaven to look down on us and our children.

Trip. (*Sullenly.*) You forget, Mrs. Triplet, that our street is very narrow, and the opposite houses are very high.

Mrs. T. James!

Trip. How can heaven see an honest man and his family in such an out-of-the-way place as this.

Mrs. T. Oh! what words are these?

Trip. Have we given honesty a fair trial? yes or no. (*Walking in great agitation*)

Mrs. T. No, not till we die as we have lived.

Trip. I *suppose* heaven is just, I can't *know* it, till it sends me an angel to take my children's part; they cry to me for bread, I have nothing to give them but hard words. God knows it has taken a great deal to break my heart, but it is broken at last, broken — broken. (*He sobs with head on his hands on table.*)

Enter WOFFINGTON, *speaking,* L. D. 2 E.

Woff. Wasn't somebody inquiring after an angel! Here I am!

Trip. Mrs. Woffington! (MRS. W. *seeing* TRIPLET's *distress, retreats; but presently comes back.*)

Woff. See. (*Shows him letter.*) "Madam, you are an angel;" from a gentleman, a perfect stranger to me, so it must be correct.

Enter POMPEY, *with a basket,* L. D. 2 E.

Ah! here is another angel! there are two sorts you know, angels of light and angels of darkness. (*Takes basket from* POMPEY.) Lucifer, avaunt! (*in a terrible tone*) and wait outside the door. (*In a familiar tone.*)   (*Exit* POMPEY L. D 2 E.)
(*Aside.*) They are in sore distress, poor things! I am sorry you are ill, Mrs. Triplet! I have brought you some physic — black draught from Burgundy. (MRS. TRIPLET *attempts to rise but sinks back again.*) Don't move I insist!

4

Trip. Oh, Mrs. Woflington, had I dreamed you would deign to come here —

Woff. You would have taken care to be out. (*Aside.*) Their faces looked pinched, I know what that means. Mrs. Triplet, I have come to give your husband a sitting for my portrait, will you allow me to eat my little luncheon in your room? I am so hungry. Pompey! (POMPEY *runs in* L. D. 2 E.) run to the corner and buy me that pie I took such a fancy to as we came along. (*Gives money to* POMPEY.)   (*Exit* POMPEY L. D. 2 E.)

Boy. Mother, will the lady give me a bit of her pie?

Mrs. T. Hush, you rude boy.

Woff. She is not much of a lady if she doesn't! Now children, we'll first look at father's comedy. Nineteen dramatis personæ, —cut out seven. Don't bring your armies into *our* drawing-rooms, Mr. Dagger and Bowl; can you marshal battalions on a Turkey carpet, and make gentlefolks witty in platoons? What's here in the first act? A duel! and both wounded — you butcher!

Trip. (*Deprecatingly.*) They are not to die, they shan't die, upon my honor!

Woff. Do you think I'll trust their lives with you? I'll show you how to run people through the body. (*Takes pen, writes.*) Business, "Araminta looks out of the garret window, the combatants drop their swords, put their hands to their hearts, and stagger off, O. P. and P. S." Now children! who helps me lay the cloth?

Chil. I, and I! (*They run to dresser.*)

Mrs. T. (*Half rising.*) Madam, I can't think of allowing you.

Woff. Sit down ma'am, or I must use brute force; (*in* MRS. T'S *ear*) shake hands with distress, for it shall never enter your door again. (MRS. T. *clasps her hands.* WOFFINGTON *meets the children with the tablecloth, which she lays.*) Twelve plates, quick! twenty-four knives, quicker! forty-eight forks, quickest.

Enter POMPEY L. D. 2 E. *who sets pie on table, and exit looking wistfully at it.*

Mr. Triplet— your coat, if you please — and carve.

Trip. My coat, madam!

Woff. Yes; off with it, there's a hole in it. (TRIPLET, *with signs of astonishment, gives her his coat, then curves pie — they eat.* WOFF. *seats herself.*) Be pleased to cast your eye on that, ma'am. (*Boy passes housewife to* MRS. TRIPLET.) Woffington's housewife, made by herself, homely to the eye, but holds everything in the world, and has a small space left for everything else; to be returned by the bearer. Thank you, sir! (*Stitches away very rapidly.*) Eat away; children, when once I begin the pie will soon end; (*girl takes plate to her mother,*) I do everything so quick.

Girl. The lady sews faster than you, mother.

Woff. Bless the child, don't come near my sword-arm, the needle will go into your eye, and out at the back of your head. (*Children laugh.*) The needle will be lost, the child will be no more, enter undertaker, house turned topsyturvy, father shows Woffington the door, off she goes, with a face as long and as dull as papa's comedy, crying, "Fine Chaney o-ran-ges!" (*The children laugh heartily.*)

Girl. Mother! the lady is very funny!

Woff. You'll be as funny when you're as well paid for it. (TRIPLET *chokes with laughing, and lays down knife and fork.*)

Mrs. T. James, take care!

Woff. There's the man's coat, (*aside*) with a ten pound note in it. (GIRL *takes it to* TRIPLET.)

Trip. My wife is a good woman, ma'am, but deficient in an important particular.

Mrs. T. Oh, James!

Trip. Yes, my dear, I regret to say you have *no sense of humor;* no more than a cat, Jane.

Woff. What! because the poor thing can't laugh at your comedy.

Trip. No ma'am, but she laughs at nothing.

Woff. Try her with one of your tragedies!

Mrs. T. I am sure, James, if I don't laugh, it is not for the want of the will. (*Dolefully*) I used to be a very heavy laughter; but I haven't laughed this two years. (WOFFINGTON *leads* MRS. T. *to chair.*)

Woff. Oh, you haven't, haven't you? Then the next two years you shall do nothing else.

Trip. Oh, madam, that passes the talent even of the great comedian.

Boy. *She* is not a comedy lady.

Woff. Hallo!

Boy. You don't ever cry, pretty lady.

Woff. (*Ironically.*) Of course not.

Boy. (*Confidentially.*) Comedy is crying. Father cries all the time he writes his comedy.

Woff. Oh!

Trip. Hold your tongue. They were tears of laughter, you know, ma'am. Wife, our children talk too much; they thrust their noses into everything, and criticise their own father.

Woff. Unnatural offsprings!

Trip. And when they take up a notion, the devil himself couldn't convince them to the contrary; for instance, all this morning they thought fit to assume that they were starving.

Boy. So we were till the angel came, and the devil went for the pie.

Trip. There, there, there, there! now, you mark my words, Jane, we shall never get that idea out of their heads —

Woff. Till we (*cuts a large piece of pie, and puts on child's plate*) put a different idea into their stomachs. Come, *trinquons!* as they do in France. (*Fills glasses, and touches hers with those of the children, who crowd round her with delight.*) Were you ever in France, Triplet?

Trip. No, madam, I am thoroughly original.

Woff. That's true. Well, I went there once to learn tragedy of the great Dumesnil. (*Recites a couple of lines of tragedy a la Française.*) But Peg Woffington was never meant to walk the stage on stilts; — no, let Mrs. Pritchard pledge Melpomene in her own poison-bowl, I'll give you Thalia in a bumper of Burgundy. Come, drink to your new mistress, Triplet. (*Fills her glass.*) Mrs. Triplet, (*she rises, bottle and glass in hand,*) I must prescribe for you too. A wine glassful of this *elixir* six times a day till further notice. Success to your husband's comedy! What's this? (*Sees fiddle in cradle.*) A fiddle, as I'm an ex-orange wench! (*Giving it to* TRIPLET.) Here, Triplet, a jig — a jig. (TRIPLET *takes fiddle.*) Peggy has not forgotten how to cover the buckle. Come, young ones — (Triplet *plays. She dances a jig with the children*) —more power to your elbow, man — shake it, ye sowl ! Hurroo ! (*She dances up to* Triplet, *who in his excitement, rises and joins in the jig, while* Mrs. Triplet *follows their movements with her body.*) But come, Mr. Triplet, you really shan't make me play the fool any longer. Business ! — my picture is to be finished. Mrs. Triplet, we must clear the studio : — take your cherubs into the bed-room.

Mrs. T. (*Seizes her hand.*) Oh, madam ! may the blessing of a mother watch over you in life and after it, and the blessing of these innocents too !

Woff. Pooh ! pooh ! let me kiss the brats. (*Kisses them. Aside.*) Poor things !

Boy. I shall pray for you after father and mother.

Girl. I shall pray for you after daily bread, because we were so hungry till you came.

Woff. (*Putting them off* R. 2 E.) There, there. Exeunt mother and cherubs. Music for the exit, Trippy — the merriest you can extort from that veteran Stradivarius of yours. (*Aside.*) Heaven knows I've as much need of merry music as the saddest of them. (*Sees* Triplet *overcome.*) Why, how now ? If there isn't this kind-hearted, soft-headed, old booby of a Triplet making a picture of himself in water colors. (*Goes up to him — taps him on the arm.*) Come ! to work — to work, and with a will, for I have invited Cibber, and Quin, and Clive, and Snarl, Soaper and all, to see the portrait, which is to make your fortune and hand me down to posterity not half as handsome as nature made me. There (*sits,*) I must put on my most bewitching smile of course. (*Aside.*) Oh, dear ! how it belies my poor aching heart.

(Triplet, *during this, has got his palette and pencil, set his easel, and begun to work, while* Woffington *sits.*) Well, are you satisfied with it ?

Trip. Anything but, madam. (*Paints.*)

Woff. Cheerful soul ! then I presume it is like.

Trip. Not a bit. (Woffington *stretches.*) You must not yawn, ma'am — you must not yawn just now !

Woff. Oh, yes, I must, if you will be so stupid.

Trip I was just about to catch the turn of the lip.

4*

Woff. Well, catch it, it wont run away.

Trip. A pleasant half-hour it will be for me, when all your friends come here, like cits at a shilling ordinary, each for his cut. Head a little more that way. (*Sadly.*) I suppose you can't sit quiet, madam ; then never mind. Look on this picture and on that !

Woff. Meaning, that I am painted as well as my picture.

Trip. Oh, no, no, no ! but to turn from your face, on which the lightning of expression plays continually, to this stony, detestable, dead daub : I could — (*seizes palette-knife*) miserable mockery ! vile caricature of life and beauty ! take that ! (*Dashes the knife through picture.*)

Woff. Oh ! right through my pet dimple ! Hark ! I hear the sound of coaches — the hour of critique approaches !

Trip. Two coach loads of criticism, and the picture ruined !

Woff. (*Reflecting.*) I'll give you a lesson — your palette-knife. (*Cuts away face of the picture.*)

Trip. There will be Mr. Cibber with his sneering snuff-box ; Mr. Quin with his humorous bludgeon ; Mrs. Clive with her tongue ; Mr. Snarl with his abuse ; and Mr. Soaper with his praise !—but I deserve it all !

Woff. That green baize — (*gets behind easel*) fling it over the easel — so ; and now (*showing her face through the picture*) you shall criticise criticism, and learn the true weight of goose's feathers. (TRIPLET *throws the baize over the picture.*)

Enter L. D. 2 E. CIBBER, CLIVE, QUIN, SNARL, *and* SOAPER.
TRIPLET *bows humbly. They return his salute carelessly.*

Cibber. Ough ! Four pair of stairs !

Quin. Well, where's the picture ? (*Crossing to* R.   *with* CLIVE. *They take up positions to look at it.*)

Trip. Mrs. Woffington, gentlemen ! (TRIPLET *removes the baize and suppresses a start.*)

Soap. Ah !

Snarl. Umph !

Quin. Ho !

Clive. Eh ?

Cibber. Ah !

Quin. Whose portrait did you say ?

Clive. He, he ! Peg Woffington's — it's a pretty head enough, and not a bit like Woffington.

Quin. Nay — compare paint with paint, Kitty — who ever saw Woffington's real face ?

Soap. Now, I call it beautiful; so smooth, polished, and uniform.

Snarl. Whereas nature delights in irregular and finely graduated surfaces. Your brush is not destitute of a certain crude talent, Mr. Triplet, but you are deficient in the great principles of Art ; the first of which is a loyal adherence to truth ; beauty itself is but one of the forms of truth, and nature is our finite exponent of infinite truth.

Soap. What wonderful criticism ! One quite loses oneself among such grand words !

Cibber. Yes, yes ! proceed, Mr. Snarl. I am of your mind.

Snarl. Now in nature, a woman's face at this distance, has a softness of outline — (*draws back and makes a lorgnette of his two hands, the others do the same,*) whereas your work is hard and tea-boardy.

Soap. Well it is a *leetle tea-boardy*, perhaps. But the light and shade, Mr. Snarl ! — the — the — what d'ye-call — the — um — you know — eh ?

Snarl. Ah ! you mean the chiaroscuro.

Soap. Exactly !

Snarl. The chiaroscuro is all wrong. In nature, the nose intercepting the light on one side the face, throws a shadow under the eye. Caravaggio, the Venetians, and the Bolognese, do particular justice to this — no such shade appears in your portrait.

Cibber. 'Tis so — stap my vitals ! (*All express assent except* Soaper.)

Soap. But my dear Mr. Snarl, if there are no shades, there are lights — loads of lights.

Snarl. There are, only they are impossible. (*Superciliously.*). You have, however, succeeded tolerably in the mechanical parts — the dress, for example ; but your Woffington is not a woman, sir — nor nature ! (*All shake their heads in assent.*)

Woff. (c.) Woman! for she has tricked four men; nature! for a fluent dunce does not know her when he sees her!

Cibber. Why — what the deuce?

Clive. Woffington!

Quin. Pheugh!

Woff. (*Steps out of picture.*) A pretty face, and not like Woffington! I owe you two, Kitty Clive. (MRS. CLIVE *bridles. To* QUIN.) Who ever saw Peggy's real face? Look at it now if you can without blushing.

All. (*Except* SNARL.) Ha! ha!

Snarl. For all this, I maintain on the unalterable rules of art —

All. Ha! ha! ha!

Snarl. (*Fiercely.*) Goths! (QUIN *and* CIBBER *turn up stage laughing.*) Good morning, ladies and gentlemen!

Cibber. Good morning, Mr. Snarl!

Snarl. I have a criticism to write of last night's performance. I shall sit on your pictures one day, Mr. Brush.

Trip. (*Crosses to* SNARL.) Pictures are not eggs, sir — they are not meant to be sat upon.

Snarl. Come, Soaper! (*Exit* L. D. 2 E.)

Soap. You shall always have my good word, Mr. Triplet.

Trip. I will try and not deserve it, Mr. Soaper!

Soap. At your service, Mr. Snarl! (*Exit* L. D. 2 E.)

Cibber. Serve 'em right — a couple of serpents! or rather one boa-constrictor — Soaper slavers, for Snarl to crush. (*Crosses to* L.) But we were all too hard on poor Trip: and if he will accept my apology —

Trip. Thank you! "Colley Cibber's Apology" can be got at any book-stall.

Cibber. Confound his impertinence! Come along, Jemmy!

Quin. If ever you paint my portrait —

Trip. The bear from Hockley Hole shall sit for the head.

Quin. Curse his impudence! Have with you, Mr. Cibber.

(*Exeunt* CIBBER *and* QUIN, L. D. 2 E.)

Clive. I did intend to have my face painted, sir, but after this —

Trip. You will continue to do it yourself!

Clive. Brute! (*Exit in a rage,* L. D. 2 E.)

Trip. Did I show a spirit, or did I not, ma'am ?

Woff. Tremendous !

Trip. Did you mark the shot I fired into each as he sheered off ?

Woff. Terrific !

Trip. I defy them ! the coxcombs ! as for real criticism, I invite it. Yours for instance, or that sweet lady's I met at Mr. Vane's, or anybody that appreciates one's beauties. By-the-bye, you were not at Mr. Vane's yesterday ?

Woff. Yes I was !

Trip. No ! I came with my verses, but she said you were not there.

Woff. Who said so ?

Trip. The charming young lady who helped me with her own hand to nectar and ambrosia.

Woff. A young lady ?

Trip. About twenty-two.

Woff. In a travelling dress ?

Trip. Yes — brown hair — blue eyes ! I poured out all to her ; — that I expected to find you; that Mr. Vane admired you; and that you were sitting to me for your portrait; that I lived at 10, Hercules Buildings, and should be proud to show her the picture for her judgment.

Woff. You told her all this ?

Trip. I did. Do you know her ?

Woff. Yes.

Trip. Who is she ?

Woff. Mrs. Vane.

Trip. Mrs. Vane ! Mr. Vane's mother ? No — no ! that can't be !

Woff. Mr. Vane's wife !

Trip. Wife ?

Woff. Yes.

Trip. Then she wasn't to know you were there ?

Woff. No.

Trip. Then I let the cat out of the bag ?

Woff. Yes.

Trip And played the devil with their married happiness ?

Woff. Probably. (*Turns her back on him.*)

Trip. Just my luck! Oh! Lord, Lord! To see what these fine gentlemen are! To have a lawful wife at home, and then to come and fall in love with you! *I* do it for ever in my plays, it is all right there!—but in real life it is abominable!

Woff. You forget, sir, that I am an actress!—a plaything for every profligate who can find the open sesame of the stage-door. Fool! to think there was an honest man in the world, and that he had shone on me!

Trip. Mrs. Woffington!

Woff. But what have we to do (*walks agitated*) with homes, and hearths, and firesides? Have we not the theatre, its triumphs, and full-handed thunders of applause? Who looks for hearts beneath the masks we wear? These men applaud us, cajole us, swear to us, lie to us, and yet, forsooth, we would have them respect us too.

Trip. (*Fiercely.*) They shall respect you before James Triplet. A great genius like you, so high above them all!—my benefactress. (*Whimpers.*)

Woff. (*Taking his hand.*) I thought this man truer than the rest. I did not feel his passion an insult. Oh! Triplet, I could have loved this man—really loved him.

Trip. Then you don't love him?

Woff. Love him! I hate him, and her, and all the world!

Trip. You will break with him then?

Woff. Break with him! No! I will feed his passion to the full—tempt him—torture him—play with him, as the angler plays the fish upon his hook! He shall rue the hour he trifled with a heart and brain like mine!

Trip. But his poor wife?

Woff. His wife! and are wives' hearts the only hearts that throb, and feel, and break? His wife must take care of herself, it is not from me that mercy can come to her.

Trip. But, madam. (*A knock at door* L. 2 E.) Who's this at such a moment. (*He goes to the window in flat.*) 'Tis a lady! Eh cloaked and hooded. Who can she be? Perhaps a sitter! My new profession has transpired! (*A tap at room-door* L. D. 2 E.)

Enter a slatternly SERVANT, *who hands a paper.*

Serv. From a lady who waits below.

Trip. (*Reads and drops the paper.*) "Mabel Vane!"

Woff. His wife here! (*To servant.*) Show the lady up stairs!
(*Exit* SERVANT, L. D. 2 E.)
What does she come here for?

Trip. I don't know, and I wish to heaven she had stayed away.
You will retire, of course you will retire?

Woff. No, sir! I will know why she comes to you. (*Reflects,
enters the picture again.*) Keep it from me if you can! (TRIPLET
sinks into a chair, the picture of consternation.)

Trip. (*With a ghastly smile, going very slowly towards the door.*) I
am going to be in the company of the two loveliest women in England; I would rather be between a lion and a unicorn — like the
royal arms. (*A tap at the door*, L. 2 E.)

Enter MABEL VANE, L. D. 2 E. *in hood and cloak, a mask in her hand.*

Trip. Madam!

Mabel. (*Crosses to* R. *hastily.*) See first that I am not followed;
that man who pursued me from my husband's house, — look out.

Trip. (*Looking through window.*) Sir Charles Pomander! — he
examines the house — his hand is on the knocker — no! he retires! (*He rids her of her hood, mantle, mask, &c.*)

Mabel. I breathe again. (*Hastily.*) Mr. Triplet, you said I
might command your services.

Trip. (*Bows.*)

Mabel. You know this actress you spoke of to-day, Mrs. Woffington?

Trip. (*Aside.*) Curse it! I am honored by her acquaintance,
madam!

Mabel. You will take me to her to the theatre where she acts?

Trip. But consider, madam!

Mabel. You must not refuse me.

Trip. But what can be the use of it?

Mabel. I am sure you are true and honest — I will trust you.
(TRIP. *bows.*) When you saw me yesterday, I was the happiest

woman in the world, for I love my husband ; and I thought then he loved me as he used to do. Two days ago I left our country home — I yearned to be by my husband's side ; I counted the hours of the journey, the miles, the yards of the road — I reached his house at last — to find that the heart, on which I had so longed to rest my head, was mine no longer.

Trip. Poor thing! poor thing!

Mabel. And she who held my place, was the woman — the actress you so praised to me; and now you pity me, do you not ; and will not refuse my request ?

Trip. But be advised ; — do not think of seeking Mrs. Woffington; she has a good heart, but a fiery temper; besides good heavens! you two ladies are rivals. Have you read the Rival Queens, madam ?

Mabel. I will cry to her for justice and mercy; — I never saw a kinder face than this lady's — she must be good and noble!

Trip. She is! I know a family she saved from starvation and despair.

Mabel. (*Seeing* WOFF. *in the picture.*) Ah! she is there! see! see! (*She approaches the easel.*)

Trip. (*Interposing.*) Oh, my portrait! you must not go near that, the colors are wet !

Mabel. Oh, that she were here, as this wonderful portrait is ; and then how I would plead to her for my husband's heart ! (*She addresses the supposed picture.*) Oh, give him back to me! what is one more heart to you ? you are so rich, and I am so poor, that without his love I have nothing ; but must sit me down and cry till my heart breaks — give him back to me, beautiful, terrible woman ; for with all your gifts you cannot love him as his poor Mabel does. Oh, give him back to me — and I will love you and kiss your feet, and pray for you till my dying day. (*Kneels to her and sobs.*) Ah ! — a tear ! it is alive ! (*Runs to* TRIPLET *and hides her head.*) I am frightened ! I am frightened !

(WOFFINGTON *steps out of frame and stands with one hand on her brow, in a half-despairing attitude. She waves her hand to* TRIPLET *to retire* — MABEL *stands trembling.*)

Woff. We would be alone.

Trip. (*In consternation.*) But, Mrs Woffington, but ladies !

Woff. Leave us!

Trip. I will retire into my sleeping apartment. (*Retires into inner room,* R. H. 2 E. *and puts out his head.*) Be composed, ladies. Neither of you could help it.

Woff. Leave us, I say ! (*He vanishes suddenly. A long uneasy pause.*)

Woff. (*With forced coldness.*) At least, madam, do me the justice to believe I did not know Mr. Vane was married.

Mabel. I am sure of it—I feel you are as good as you are gifted.

Woff. Mrs. Vane, I am not—you deceive yourself.

Mabel. Then, Heaven have mercy on me ! but you are—I see it in your face, ah! you know you pity me !

Woff. I do, madam—and I could consent never more to see your—Mr. Vane.

Mabel. Ah ! but will you give me back his heart ? What will his presence be to me if his love remain behind ?

Woff. But, how, madam ?

Mabel. The magnet can repel as well as attract — you who can enchant — can you not break your own spell ?

Woff. You ask much of me !

Mabel. Alas, I do !

Woff. But I could do even this.

Mabel. You could !

Woff. And perhaps if you — who have not only touched my heart, but won my respect, say to me — "do so," I shall do it. (*Mabel clasps her hands.*) There is only one way — but that way is simple. Mr. Vane thinks better of me than I deserve — I have only to make him (*with a trembling lip,*) believe me worse than I am, and he will return to you, and love you better, far better, for having known, admired, and despised Peg Woffington.

Mabel. Oh ! I shall bless you every hour of my life. (*Pause.*) But rob you of your good name ! bid a woman soil her forehead so for me ! (*Sighs, long pause.*) With Heaven's help I do refuse your offer; it is better I should die with my heart crushed, but my conscience unstained ; for so my humble life has passed till now.

Woff. Humble ! such as you are the diamonds of the world!!!

5

Angel of truth and goodness, you have conquered! The poor heart we both overrate shall be your's again. In my hands 'tis painted glass at best — but set in the lustre of your love, it may become a priceless jewel. Can you trust me?

Mabel. With my life!

Woff. And will you let me call you friend?

Mabel. Friend! no — not friend!

Woff. Alas!

Mabel. Let me call you sister! I have no sister! (*Timidly and pleadingly.*)

Woff. Sister! oh, yes! call me sister! (*They embrace.*) You do not know what it is to me, whom the proud ones of the world pass by with averted looks, to hear that sacred name from lips as pure as yours. Let me hold you in my arms — so — a little while — if you knew the good it does me to feel your heart beating close to mine; (*pause*) and now to bring back this truant — how this heart flutters — you must compose yourself. (*Goes to door* R. 2 E. *leading to inner room and opens it.*) And I have need to be alone awhile. (*Puts her in, comes forward and sits a moment with her hands pressed over her forehead.*) 'Twas a terrible wrench — but 'tis over; and now — "about my brains," as Hamlet says — to bring back the husband to his duty — what a strange office for a woman like me! How little the world knows about us after all. (*She sighs and sobs convulsively.*) I ought to feel very happy — pshaw! On with the mask and spangles, Peggy — and away with the fumes of this pleasant day-dream — how to bring Pomander hither? Let me see — this paper — (*takes paper* MABEL *sent up*) signed in her hand; Mabel Vane — what if by its aid — I have it — pen — ink — one never can find writing materials in an author's room (*Goes to door and calls.*) Triplet!

Enter TRIPLET *from inner room* R. 2 E.

Pens and ink — quick!

Trip. (*Gets them, looking at her.*) Here, madam — and paper!

Woff. No, I have that here. (*She writes — he watches her.*)

Trip. Her eyes are red — and Mrs. Vane all of a flutter inside. There's been a storm — but they haven't torn each other in pieces, that's one comfort. But has she relented, I wonder.

Woff. Triplet! This note to Sir Charles Pomander.

Trip. Madam! (*Takes it.*) What is it, I wonder? However, 'tis not my business. (*Going — pauses.*) But it is my business — I'm not a postman — if I carry letters I ought to know the contents. (*Returns.*) Madam —

Woff. Well!

Trip. Madam — I — I —

Woff. I see — you wish to know the contents of that letter — hear them: " Follow the bearer."

Trip. Madam!

Woff. (*Reads.*) I am here without my husband's knowledge.

Trip. Mrs. Woffington!

Woff. (*Reads.*) Alone and unprotected — signed "Mabel Vane."

Trip. Her own signature, too! Mrs. Woffington — you are a great actress — you have been cruelly wronged — you have saved me from despair, and my children from starvation; but before I will carry that letter, I will have my hands hacked off at the wrists.

Woff. (*Aside.*) What a good creature this is. Then you refuse to obey my orders.

Trip. No! no! ask me to jump out of that window — to burn my favorite tragedy — to forswear pen and ink for ever — anything but carry that letter, and I will do it.

Woff. Well — leave the letter! (TRIPLET *runs for his hat.*) Where are you going?

Trip. To bring the husband to his wife's feet — and so to save one angel — that's the lady in the other room — from despair; and another angel — that's you, from a great crime. Trust poor Jemmy Triplet for once to bring this domestic drama to a happy denouement! (*Exit* L. D. 2 E.)

Woff. How innocently he helps my plot! I must have all the puppets under my hand. If I know Sir Charles, he is still on the watch. (*Goes to window in flat.*) Yes! (*Goes to inner door* 2 E. R.) Here — your eldest boy, Mrs. Triplet; I want him.

Enter LYSIMACHUS R. 2 E.

Lysimachus, you see that gentleman, run down — give him this

letter — and the show him up here. (*Exit* LYSIMACHUS L. 2 E.,
And now Mrs. Vane's mantle, the hood well forward — so — we
are nearly of a height — he does not know I am here — if I can
but imitate her voice and rustic shyness — *allons*, Peggy, 'tis seldom you acted in so good a cause. (*She assumes the air of* MRS.
VANE.)

Enter POMANDER L. D. 2 E. WOFFINGTON *appears sunk in
grief—he comes forward—she starts and gives a little shriek.*

Pom. My dear Mrs. Vane. (*She shrinks.*) Do not be alarm-
ed — loveliness neglected, and simplicity deceived, give irresistible
claims to respect as well as adoration. Had fate given me this
hand. (*He takes her hand.*)

Woff. Oh, please, sir !

Pom. Would I have abandoned it for that of a Woffington —
as artificial and hollow a jade as ever winked at a side-box.
Oh, had I been your husband, madam — how would I have re-
velled in the pastoral pleasures you so sweetly recalled yesterday—
the Barbary mare —

Woff. (*Timidly.*) Hen !

Pom. Ah, yes, the Barbary hen; and old dame — dame —

Woff. Best, please, sir !

Pom. Yes, best — that happy though elderly female for whom
you have condescended to make puddings.

Woff. Alas, sir !

Pom. You sigh ! It is not yet too late to convert me. Upon
this white hand I swear to become your pupil, as I am your
adorer. (*He kisses it.*) Let me thus fetter it with a worthy mana-
cle. (*Aside.*) What will innocence say to my five hundred guinea
diamond ?

Woff. La, sir ! how pretty !

Pom. Let me show how poor its lustre is to that of your eyes
(*He tries to draw back her hood.*)

Woff. Oh, sir — hark ! (*She suddenly starts away, and listens in
an attitude of alarm.*)

Pom. Ah ! (*Noise without 2 E. L.*) Footsteps on the stairs!
(*Goes to door R. E. L. and opens it, listening.*)

Vane. (*Without.*) Another flight!

Pom. Ha! Vane's voice, by all 's mal-à-propos — (Wor-
FINGTON *screams and rushes into inner apartment* 2 E. R.) and now
for Monsieur le mari. (TRIPLET *appears at the door* 2 E. L. H.
with his back to the stage and speaking off \

Trip. Have a care, sir! There is a hiatus in the fourth step —
and now for the friend who waits to forget grief and suspicion in
your arms — that friend is —

Enter VANE, D. 2 E. L. TRIPLET *turns round and recognises* Po-
MANDER, *who is on* R. H.

The Devil!

Pom. You flatter me!

Vane. So this is the mysterious rencontre — pray, Sir Charles,
what is it you want to forget in my arms?

Pom. In your arms! (*Aside.*) Confounds himself with his wife.
Perhaps you had better explain, my friend?

Trip. Nay, sir — be yours the pleasing duty!

Vane. In one word, Sir Charles Pomander, why are you here?
and for what purpose am I sent for?

Pom. In two words, my dear fellow, I don't choose to tell you
why I am here — and 'twas not I who sent for you.

Vane. (*To* TRIPLET.) Speak, sirrah — your riddling message!

Trip. There's nothing for it but the truth. Then, sir — the
'nd I expected you would find here was Mrs. ——

1 n. (*To* TRIPLET.) Stop, my deplorable-looking friend:
(*to* VANE) when the answer to such a question begins with a mistress, I think you had better not inquire further. (*To* TRIP.)
Don't complete the name.

Vane. I command you to complete it, or —

Trip. Gentlemen, gentlemen, how am I to satisfy both of
you?

Pom. My dear Vane, remember it is a lady's secret — the only
thing in the world one is bound to keep, except one's temper,
which by-the-bye, you're losing rapidly.

Vane. (*Aside.*) He spoke of griefs and suspicions to be forgiven
and forgotten. Mabel has left my house. (*Crosses to* c.) Sir
5*

Charles Pomander, I insist on knowing who this lady is. If it be as I fear, I have the best right to ask.

Pom. But the worst right to be answered.

Vane. How am I to construe this tone, sir ?

Pom. Do as we did at school with a troublesome passage — don't construe it at all.

Vane. Sir Charles Pomander, you are impertinent.

Pom. My dear Vane, you are in a passion.

Vane. By heaven, sir —

Trip. Gentlemen, gentlemen, I give you my word, Mr. Vane, she does not know of Sir Charles Pomander's presence here.

Vane. She ? s'death, who ?

Trip. Mrs. Vane!

Vane. My wife — here and with him ?

Trip. No — not with *him!*

Pom. I regret to contradict you, my dilapidated friend, or to hurt you, my dear Vane; but really, in self-defence — you know this signature. (*Offers paper written by* WOFFINGTON.)

Vane. Mabel's hand !

Pom. Yes — what my attentions began, your little peccadillo finished — cause and effect, my dear fellow — pure cause and effect.

Vane. Coxcomb and slanderer ! draw and defend yourself. (*Draws.*)

Pom. If you will have it! (*Draws.*)

Trip. (*Throwing himself between them.*) Hold ! hold !

(WOFFINGTON *suddenly presents herself at the threshold of the door* 2 E. R. H. *her hood is drawn over her face.*)

Trip. Mrs. Vane !

Vane. Mabel ! wife ! say that this is not true — that you were lured by stratagem. Oh, speak ! belie this coxcomb ! You know how bitterly I repented the infatuation that brought me to the feet of another.

(WOFFINGTON *bursts into a laugh, and throws back the hood.*)

Pom. Woffington !

Vane. She here !

Woff. There, Sir Charles, did I not wager he would confess he was heartily ashamed of himself ? (*Crosses to* C.)

Trip. (*Aside.*) I have a glimmer of comprehension.

Woff. Yes—we have had our laugh—and Mr. Vane his lesson; as for Mrs. Vane—this way, madam, and satisfy yourself.

MABEL *enters* D. R. 2 E.

Mabel. Ernest—dear Ernest!

Vane. (*Sternly.*) Mabel, how came you here?

Woff. In such very questionable company as a town rake and a profane stage-player? Mrs. Vane might have asked the same question yesterday. Why Mrs. Vane somehow fancied you had mislaid your heart in Covent Garden green-room, and that I had feloniously appropriated it; she came here, in search of stolen goods—would you could rummage here, madam, and satisfy yourself if you still want proof, that I have no such thing as a heart about me—not even one of my own.

Trip. I deny that—a better heart than Mrs. Woffington's—'

Woff. What on earth do you know about it, man?

Vane. (*To* MABEL.) But this letter?

Woff. Was written by me on a paper which by accident bore Mrs. Vane's signature. The fact is, I had a wager with Sir Charles here—his diamond ring against my left-hand glove—that I could bewitch a certain country gentleman's imagination, though his heart all the while belonged to its rightful owner, and I have won. (*Sighs.*)

Vane. What a dupe I have been—am I enough humiliated?

Pom. Ha! ha! ha! My poor fellow, you had better return to Huntingdonshire, and leave town and the players to us, who know how to deal with them.

Woff. And are quite safe against being taken in—eh! Sir Charles? (*Points to ring on her finger.*)

Pom. Oh, perfectly—we know each other's cards—retain that ring as a mark of my—(WOFF. *holds up her finger*) respect!

Woff. No, no—I accept your ring; but I shall always hate you.

Pom. I welcome the sentiment—I can endure anything but your indifference.

Vane. And you, Mabel, will you forgive my infatuation?

Mabel. I forgive all, Ernest. (*Crosses to* WOFFINGTON, *aside to her.*) What do we not owe you sister ?

Woff. Nothing that word does not pay for. (*Aside.*) Alas ! and so ends the game. You and I have the tricks, I think, Sir Charles — Mrs. Vane the honors. — Mr. Vane will quit hazard and the clubs for Willoughby Manor and the double dummy of a matrimonial rubber. As for me, I revoke my lead of hearts.

Pom. After taking my ace of diamonds !

Trip. And poor Jemmy Triplet I suppose must once again take up his solitary hand at patience.

Woff. Unless Manager Rich is fool enough to accept my judgment for gospel — and then — but whom have we here ?

Enter D. 2 E. L. H. CIBBER, QUIN, MRS. CLIVE, SNARL, *and* SOAPER. SNARL *and* SOAPER *cross behind to* R. H.

Cibber. Ah ! Mrs. Vane — Mr. Vane — Sir Charles — Peggy — Bonjour, Mesdames et Messieurs — Mr. Triplet, I congratulate you — stap my vitals !

Trip. Congratulate me !

Clive. Yes — Quin here, who's a good natured bear, declares we behaved shamefully to you to-day, and so as Mr. Rich has just told us of your good fortune —

Trip. My good fortune ! there must be some mistake. You've come to the wrong house.

Quin. No ; you have a prospect henceforward of dining every day of your life. 'Tis a great comfort, and I wish you appetite to enjoy it, Mr. Triplet.

Trip. Am I awake ? Pinch me, somebody — (WOFFINGTON *pinches him*) — thank you — I *am* awake.

Cibber. Manager Rich, thanks to Peggy's influence here, and a good word or two from one who shall be nameless, has accepted one of your tragedies..

Trip. Oh, Lord !

Soap. He ! he ! I give you joy, Mr. Triplet ; Mr. Snarl and I are so glad, for as Mr. Snarl said to me, as we left your studio this morning, "I do so wish they'd play one of Mr. Triplet's tragedies."

Snarl. That I might have the pleasure of criticising it. Mr. Rich did me the honor to ask which of the three we should accept — I told him, the shortest.

Clive. You'll be pleased to hear, Mrs. Woffington, there's a capital part for *me*. (*Aside.*) Now she could knock me down, I know.

Trip. One of my tragedies accepted at last! Oh, gracious goodness! Break it gently to my wife — I know I'm dreaming, but prithee don't anybody wake me. Oh, Mrs. Woffington — my guardian angel — my preserver! (*Seizes her hand.*)

Woff. No, no — we had better wait, and see on which act of your tragedy the curtain falls.

Trip. Ah! I forgot that.

Mabel. I need not wait to express my gratitude — say in what way can I ever thank you?

Woff. Dear sister, when hereafter in your home of peace you hear harsh sentence passed on us, whose lot is admiration, but rarely love, triumph but never tranquility — think sometimes of poor Peg Woffington, and say, stage masks may cover honest faces, and hearts beat true beneath a tinselled robe.

Nor ours the sole gay masks that hide a face
Where care and tears have left their withering trace,
On the world's stage, as in our mimic art,
We oft confound the actor with the part.
    Pom. Distrust appearances — an obvious moral —
With which, however, I've no time to quarrel;
Though for my part, I've found, the winning riders
In the world's race are often the outsiders.
    Vane. So I have played at love — witched from my will.
    Mabel. My love was always Ernest, and is still.
    Cibber Pshaw! stap my vitals! "Manners make the man,"
They have made *me!*
    Snarl.   'T is about all they can!
    Soap. Yes; Mr. Cibber's epitaph shall be,
He played Lord Foppington at seventy-three.
    Clive. I'm for plain speaking — let the truth be shown —
    Snarl. Truth's in a well — best leave that well alone —

Quin.   Its bitter waters why should *you* uncork?
No; play like me — an honest knife and fork.
   Trip.   That part would be well played by many a poet,
Had he the practice one must have, to know it,
But 'tis the verdict by the public past,
Must sentence scribblers or to feast or fast.
Be kind to-night: in triplet tone I sue,
As actor, manager, and author too.
   Pom.   Mind that for sentence when they call the cause on,
You've at least one Peg here — to hang applause on.
   Woff.   Yes; sure those kind eyes and bright smiles one traces
Are not deceptive *masks* — but honest *faces.*
I'd swear it — but if your hands make it certain,
Then all is right on both sides of the curtain.

SITUATIONS.

WOFFINGTON.
VANE.   TRIPLET.
MRS. VANE.   CIBBER.
SIR CHAS.   MRS. CLIVE.
SOAPER.   QUIN.
SNARL.

R. H.   L. H.

THE END.

COSTUME.

Sir Charles. — Scarlet square cut coat, gold holes; amber silk breeches; rich, long vest; white silk stockings, drawn over the knee; black shoes with high red heels; diamond buckles; small three-cornered hat, fringed with feathers; long flaxen wig, tied in large queue at back; ruffles; dress steel sword, and stick. *Second Dress.* Amber silk embroidered square cut coat, (for Scene 2) rest of dress as Scene 1.

Ernest Vane. —· Bright plum silk velvet square cut coat, and breeches; long white satin vest, gold holes to the suit; white silk stockings, drawn over the knee; black shoes, with high red heels, diamond buckles; small three cornered hat, fringed with feathers; long brown wig, tied in a large queue at back; ruffles; dress steel sword, and stick.

Colley Cibber. — Light brown square coat and breeches; rose colored vest; white silk stockings, drawn over the knees; black shoes, with high red heels, diamond buckles; small three-cornered hat, fringed with feathers; white powdered bag wig; ruffles, and dress steel sword. (A mild edition of his own Lord Foppington.) Sallow face, described as of wash leather.

Quin. — Fawn square cut coat and breeches; rose colored vest; white silk stockings, drawn over the knee; black shoes, high red heels, diamond buckles; small three-cornered hat, fringed with feathers; powdered bag wig; ruffles, and dress steel sword.

Triplet. — Black square cut coat and breeches; dark vest; gray stockings; black shoes and buckles; three-cornered hat; brown wig, with large queue tied at back, (dressed seedy;) a hole under the arm at coat.

Lysimachus. — Dark square cut coat and breeches; dark vest and stockings; black shoes, (dressed seedy.)

Mr. Snarl. — Dark blue square cut coat, and breeches, small silver holes; embroidered vest; appointments same as Colley Cibber.

Mr. Soaper. — Green square cut coat and breeches; gold holes; embroidered vest; appointments same as Snarl.

James Burdock. — Square cut livery coat, breeches and vest; old fashioned boots; old man's silver-haired wig.

Colander. — Black velvet square cut coat and breeches; embroidered vest; silk stockings; black shoes and buckles; bag wig; patches on face; well appointed in the height of fashion, no sword.

Handsdon. — Rich square cut livery buttoned up the front; breeches, buff belt and buckle; high black boots and shins; three-cornered hat and bag wig.

Call Boy. — Plain square cut coat, breeches; stockings, shoes, and bag wig.

Pompey. — Turkish trowsers; crimson Jacket, and fly trimmed with gold lace; red slippers; turban; black face and black wig; page after Hogarth's marriage a La Mode.

Mrs. Vane. — *First Dress.* Travelling green skirt and cardinal. *Second Dress.* Plain silk brocade, full at hips, not hooped; short sleeves laced; caned hood and cape; (black silk) called cardinal.

Peg. — *First Dress.* Rich silk dress, pearl white, with flowers and sprig embroidered; neck and arms bare. *Second Dress.* Handsome dinner dress, same period. *Third Dress.* Walking dress, with black cardinal.

Kitty Clive. — Gaudy dress, same period, stripe damask.

Mrs. Triplet. — Shally dress, same period.

Roxalana. — Shally dress (child), same period

Maid. — Shally dress.

Period, 1750. *Reign of George Third.*

The young men wore their own hair long and tied up in a queue behind. The elder retained the powdered wig.

The ladies, wore their hair completely thrown back, and tied at back in a arge broad queue.

The above dresses are from prints of the time, in the possession of Alfred Howell, Esq., Costumer of the Boston Theatre.

A Glorious Change.

Medical treatment has been revolutionized. The Drastic purgatives with which it was the fashion to scour the system for every ailment, twenty years ago, have been abandoned. At last the discovery has been made that RENOVATION, NOT PROSTRATION, IS THE TRUE MEDICAL PHILOSOPHY. The introduction of *PLANTATION BITTERS* opened the eyes of the world to this great fact. The life-sustaining principle embodied in this great Vegetable Restorative is manifested in the weak and desponding by an immediate and most encouraging change. A pleasant glow, the precursor of returning health, is diffused through the system, and every day the invalid is conscious of a new accession of vital power. If the appetite has failed, it is quickened; if digestion has been painful and imperfect, it becomes easy and thorough; if the liver is torpid, it is roused and regulated, if the nerves are relaxed, they are strengthened and restrung; if the brain has been haunted by morbid fancies, they are put to flight, and hope and cheerfulness return. The old practice was to convulse, and rack, and strain the feeble patient with powerful cathartics. It was like clubbing a man after he was down. Happily, this false and fatal mode of treatment no longer finds favor with the enlightened members of the faculty. In the face of the extraordinary cures of general debility, dyspepsia, biliousness, constipation and mental despondency, wrought by Plantation Bitters, no practitioner, not in league with death and the undertaker, could persist in it. The terrible evacuents which were once prescribed as Spring and Summer Medicines, have utterly lost their *prestige*. The sick will not take them—and Plantation Bitters, in which are combined the elements of a stomachic, an invigorant, a mild laxative, a nervine, and an anti-bilious specific, reigns in their stead. Plantation Bitters are sold by all respectable Druggists in the United States.

THE NEW FOOD.

Office of the RAND SEA MOSS FARINE CO.,
No. 53 PARK PLACE.

In order that the public may be as fully informed as possible, in regard to the Sea Moss Farine, we submit as much information of its worth and merit as space will admit. It is exceedingly gratifying to the Company to know that their efforts to place a really good article of food in the market is so fully appreciated ; and we trust that in the future, as well as in the past, we may continue to merit the appreciation of all.

[From the Weekly Tribune of Dec. 15, 1869.]

AMERICAN INSTITUTE FARMERS' CLUB,

Session of December 7, 1869, held at Cooper Union. Alderman Nathan C. Ely in the chair, John W. Chambers, Secretary. The first subject introduced was—

"A NEW ARTICLE OF FOOD."

The "ex-Mayor of Boston," Hon. J. V. C. Smith, M. D., distributed some parcels of SEA MOSS FARINE which he said is offered to the public as the most nutritive, delicious and cheap article of its class ever manufactured in this country or in Europe. The ex-Mayor gave a lengthened professiona evidence in favor of the preparation, and detailed like opinions of medical gentlemen in Europe.

To ascertain if these claims are well founded, the following ladies—who are distinguished for their intelligence and social position, and as acting under the authority of the Institute—were appointed a Committee to examine it and report : Mrs. L. E. Lyman, Mrs. J. W. Chambers, Mrs. D. T. Conner, Mrs. D. B. Bruen and Mrs. M. J. Cushing, M. D.

[From the Weekly Tribune, Dec. 22, 1869.]

AMERICAN INSTITUTE FARMERS' CLUB,

Session of Tuesday, Dec. 21, 1869, held at Cooper Union. Nathan C. Ely, Chairman ; John W. Chambers, Secretary.

Report on the New Article of Food—Sea Moss Farine.

The Committee of Ladies, Mrs. Lyman, Mrs. Chambers and others, requested to report on Carrageen, or Irish Moss (from which SEA MOSS FARINE is manufactured), as a dish for the table, finds that the substance grows on rocks and stones on the sea-coasts of Europe, and in peculiar abundance on the Atlantic coast of Ireland, where it is chiefly gathered. It is said to be a native of the United States, and is found in limited quantities on the coast of Massachusetts. It is picked from the rocks at low tide. After being washed, it is dried in the sun. Chemists and doctors who have analyzed it, find it is nutritive and demulcent ; and, being easy of digestion, it forms a useful article of diet as a substitute for grain foods, and is particularly recommended in chronic pectoral affections, scrofulous complaints, dysentery, diarrhea, &c. Carrageen is very gelatinous, and very valuable as food. It is recognized as superior to all orders of moss as demulcent, and in its nutritive qualities. It is said that Napoleon Bonaparte said to Dr. O'Meara, at St. Helena, that it was employed as an article of diet by physicians in Corsica, in the treatment of tumors and cancers, on account of the iodine it contains. It is used in England and France as a light and nourishing article of food.

A NEW FOOD SOURCE.

The moss, as it comes from the sea, is filled with sand, pebbles, small shells, &c., and very saline in taste : and, prepared as food in its original state, is very troublesome to the housekeeper, while it is very easy to prepare when made from SEA MOSS FARINE. By this process, it is first thoroughly washed and deprived of its extreme saline taste. It is then picked over by hand and desiccated, after which it passes through several mills and machines, by which it is cleaned perfectly, and reduced to a powdered and concentrated condition without being deprived of its refreshing ocean flavor. A packet of Corn Starch, Maizena or Farina costs 10c. at retail, and makes, combined with milk, without eggs, only from four to six quarts of Blanc Mange Pudding, while SEA MOSS FARINE, costing 25c., will produce full sixteen quarts. The Committee are satisfied that as a cheap, simple and ready dessert, or a dish for young children and for invalids, it will be found, *as thus prepared*, a valuable addition to articles more generally known and widely used.

(Signed,)

MRS. L. E. LYMAN, (wife of the Agricultural Editor of the N. Y. Tribune.
MRS. J. W. CHAMBERS, (wife of the Secretary of the American Institute.)
MRS. D. T. CONNER, 5-Mile Run, N. J.
MRS. D. B. BRUEN, Newark, N. J.
MRS. MARIA J. CUSHING, M. D., 231 East 40th St., N. Y.

ASTOR HOUSE, NEW YORK, Jan., 1870.

RAND SEA MOSS FARINE CO.:
    Gentlemen : We commenced the use of your Sea Moss Farine at your earnest solicitation, but very reluctantly, and without any faith in it, from the fact that so many new articles of food are daily offered, and prove, in almost every case, to be utterly worthless. We are very happy to say that yours has not only proved an exception, but is a *decided success*. It not only possesses *real merit,* but makes a *delicious dessert*. We shall continue to use it for two reasons: *first,* the guests of the Astor House like it ; and *second, we like it, because it is by far the cheapest article in the market* for Blanc Mange, Puddings, Creams, &c.

Very respectfully yours,
C. A. STETSON'S SONS

BROOKLYN, N. Y., Sept. 13, 1869.

    My Dear Rand : I have submitted your "Sea Moss Farine" to the "kitchen cabinet," and the decision is decidedly favorable. It quite surpassed my most sanguine expectations. There is a slight and yet positive sea flavor—just a hint of the ocean—in it, which is rare and delightful. My wife liked it, the children liked it—took to it naturally—and all at the table passed up their dishes twice. The peoples' proverb was verified, that *"the proof of a pudding is in eating it."*

Your friend and brother,
J. HYATT SMITH,
Pastor of the Lee Ave. Baptist Church.

PARKER HOUSE, BOSTON, Jan. 25, 1870.

RAND SEA MOSS FARINE CO., New York :
    We are using "Sea Moss Farine," and find it just what you state it is—real, pure Irish Moss, so refined, desiccated and condensed that we can prepare dishes for dessert from it in a few minutes, instead of hours, when made from the crude moss.
    We very cordially recommend it (as prepared by you) far superior and much cheaper than Corn Starch, Maizena, Farina, Gelatine, or any like article for Blanc Mange, Creams, Puddings, Charlotte Russe, &c., &c. We hope that its delicate and elegant appearance on the table—and more than all this, its well-known healthfulness and delicious flavor—will command for it millions of consumers.

Respectfully yours,
H. D. PARKER & CO.

A NEW FOOD SOURCE.

We have received the following characteristic note from the celebrated Dio Lewis, A. M., M. D., Principal of the Lexington Young Ladies' Seminary for Physical Education, author of "Weak Lungs, and How to Make Them Strong," of "The New Gymnastics for Men, Women and Children," and "Lecture on Physical Culture :"

17 Beacon Street, Boston, January 25, 1870.

RAND SEA MOSS FARINE CO.:

My wife says that your new preparation, "Sea Moss Farine," is *worth its weight in GOLD* ; *no trouble, so sure,* and so *delicious*.

Believe me, in addition to my "better half's" testimony, when I add that my *most toothsome tooth* is very thankfully yours. DIO LEWIS.

FROM THE PRESS.

No such sensation has been created in the food market during the present century, as that occasioned by the introduction of the *new staff of life*, known as Sea Moss Farine. It is difficult to tell the truth about this extraordinary article of diet without being suspected of exaggeration.—*Boston Post.*

A still greater number of distinguished physicians and scientific chemists indorse it as a nutrient of the very first class, while every housekeeper who uses it admits that it is fully fifty per cent. cheaper than Maizena, Farina, Corn Starch, or any other kindred preparation.—*Boston Times.*

Housekeepers declare that the quantity of exquisite Custards, Blanc Mange, Light Pudding, Creams, Jelly, &c., producible from the Farine, exceeds by one half that obtainable from any other glutinous agent used in cooking.—*St. Louis Republican.*

One experiment will convince the most skeptical that with Sea Moss Farine they can produce unequalled Custards, Puddings, Jellies, Charlotte Russe, Creams, Soups, &c., &c.—*Express.*

Here, then, we have an entirely new article of food of the most delicate and inviting character, adapted to the use of the table for Blanc Mange, Puddings, Charlotte de Russe, &c., and almost invaluable for use by the invalid. It is simple, delicate, nutritious, harmless, remedial and economical, as it can be furnished for one-third to one-half the cost of Corn Starch, Maizena, Farina, &c., for all of which it is more than a substitute. It is made up without trouble, and will always be good. Try it ; and our word for it, you will continue in its use.—*Independent.*

The Company state at least fifty delicious dishes can be made from the Sea Moss Farine, and give in their circular the recipes for many of them. We consider Mr. Rand's discovery a highly-important one for the millions, and indeed for all classes of society, in these stringent times.—*The Weekly.*

It has been placed, so to speak, in the front rank of our food staples, and all that has been said of it by the patentee (Mr. Rand), and the Company interested in its sale, appears to be approved and confirmed by public opinion.—*The Mail.*

As to its deliciousness, the "proof of the pudding is in eating it ;" and we feel confident that no man or woman who has once eaten of a Blanc Mange, Pudding, Custard, Cream, Charlotte Russe, or any other delicacy prepared with this marine Godsend, will deny its claim to rank among the table luxuries of the period.—*Tribune.*

This apparently impossibility has been overcome—experimental science overcomes almost every obstacle, now-a-days—and Irish Moss, purified, concentrated, and rendered an absolute luxury, as SEA MOSS FARINE, will hereafter be quoted as a food staple in the markets of the world.—*The World.*

Hence it will be cheap as long as the sea and rocks last—which will be long enough for all practicable purposes. Our main object in this article has been to place what we believe to be a subject of great importance, in its true light ; nothing more, nothing less.—*Home Journal.*